ONE BAD DECISION

ONE BAD DECISION

THE UNBELIEVABLE MR. BROWNSTONE™ BOOK TEN

MICHAEL ANDERLE

DISRUPTIVE IMAGINATION

THE ONE BAD DECISION TEAM

Special Thanks
to Mike Ross
for BBQ Consulting
Jessie Rae's BBQ - Las Vegas, NV

Thanks to the JIT Readers

Mary Morris
John Ashmore
James Caplan
Thomas Ogden
Kelly O'Donnell
Peter Manis
Paul Westman
Daniel Weigert
Micky Cocker
Larry Omans

If I've missed anyone, please let me know!

Editor
Lynne Stiegler

To Family, Friends and
Those Who Love
to Read.
May We All Enjoy Grace
to Live the Life We Are
Called.

Debbie wrinkled her nose as an acrid odor escaped the wide-bottomed bottle sitting on the counter in front of her. She sighed and lifted a beaker filled with glowing azure liquid and poured it into the frothy mixture in the bottle. The stench grew stronger, forcing her to back up.

She coughed and waved her hand in front of her face. "Damn, this crap smells bad. Hope my neighbors just assume I'm smoking pot again."

There'd been far too many close calls with the police lately. She wasn't sure how much longer she could stay in the apartment, as much as she enjoyed the location.

The doorbell rang, and a soft knock followed.

Debbie rolled her eyes. "I hate it when clients show up early. Late I understand, but early? You'll mess up my spells. If you're paying for quality, you have to give me the *time* for quality, idiots."

She wanted to give them a piece of her mind, but her

clients weren't the kind of men you risked casually insulting.

The witch made her way to the door after another soft knock. She reached over and pulled the door open, fully expecting a few not-so-fine gentlemen from the local Russian Mafia.

Nope. Not her clients, but a broad-shouldered well-muscled black man in a suit and sunglasses. A platinum-blonde teenage girl watched from several yards back.

Debbie tilted her head. It was almost as if the girl's hair wasn't blonde, but white, with the black at the roots. Months overdue for a new dye job, apparently.

The witch narrowed her eyes. She shouldn't be worrying about the hair color of some random girl. She needed to figure out who these people were and get rid of them before her clients showed up. The combination of the man in a suit and the girl suggested religious proselytizers.

She needed many things in life. Religion wasn't one of them.

The man cleared his throat. "You Debbie?"

The witch frowned. Maybe not religious nuts after all, or maybe knowing her name was part of their conversion strategy.

"Who are you?" she demanded. "I'm very busy right now, so I don't have time to buy whatever it is that you're selling or take whatever pamphlets you're offering. I also don't vote, and I don't sign petitions."

The man laughed. "You're just a real pillar of the community, ain't you, Debbie?"

"Go away. Now."

"I'm afraid I can't do that, ma'am. I'm Shorty. I'm with

the Brownstone Agency." He reached up to adjust his tie. "You have a level two bounty on you for illegal distribution of controlled substances, including dust." He smiled. "Come along quietly, and we can go down to the station all nice and peaceful like. I don't like getting rough with ladies, even when they are criminals, so be nice, okay?"

Debbie scoffed. A bounty hunter. An idiot bounty hunter who had underestimated her at that. She didn't share his concerns about hurting people, man or woman. Her hand drifted toward her pocket.

"Shorty, be careful, I can see magi—" the girl behind him called.

The witch ripped a small glass vial out of her pocket and threw it at Shorty. The bounty hunter leapt to the side. The vial smashed against the cement right behind him, a thick cloud of green smoke billowing out. Debbie slammed and locked the door.

"What the fuck is that smell?" Shorty yelled from the other side. Thick smoke infiltrated the apartment underneath the door. "Shit." He coughed.

"He needs help," the girl yelled.

She shouldn't have come along with bounty hunters if she didn't want to see anyone get hurt. Stupid little blonde chick.

The witch dashed into her bedroom and then her walk-in closet. She grabbed a large satchel out of her closet, her running-away bag. She hated to leave all her reagents and other supplies behind, but bounty hunters were a lot like ants or roaches; when you saw one, several others were always near.

The witch sprinted toward the back door and threw it

open. There was no way she was letting Shorty and his little friend take her anywhere, and she wasn't waiting for his friends to show up.

She jerked to a stop, almost falling over.

Another bounty hunter stood on her back porch in a nearly matching suit and glasses. That was annoying enough, but he was a minor concern at that moment. Her gaze locked on the man several yards behind him, the real threat.

Mottled face. Ridiculous muscles that strained his shirt. Tattoo-covered arms.

"Brownstone," Debbie hissed.

She didn't understand why he was there. Her bounty was far too low for the Granite Ghost to care. Everyone said he didn't get out of bed for less than a level three anymore, and most of the time even those weren't enough for him.

The first bounty hunter had mentioned a Brownstone Agency. What was that? Some sort of franchise?

The witch took a few steps back as the first bounty hunter grinned at her.

"Don't worry about Brownstone. He's just here as kind of an observer. *I'm* your problem. My name is Trey Garfield, and I'm taking you in. Turn around and put your hands behind your back, and this won't be a big deal at all. I figure, you don't start anything, I'm not gonna start anything. Fair is fair, you know what I'm saying?"

The witch lurched to the side and pulled out another vial. She threw it at Trey's feet and ran. The man grunted and jumped back, a small explosion shredding the front of his suit jacket and the rocks in the yard doing a number on his pants as he landed and rolled.

"I just bought this suit, you bitch," he shouted. He patted the burning fabric of his jacket.

The witch rushed back toward the front of her apartment. The noxious fumes from the earlier vial should have already sunken to the ground, and Shorty wouldn't be in any position to stop her. She unlocked and pulled open the door, expecting to see a choking and coughing bounty hunter.

The man was sitting on the ground several yards away, leaning against a Ford F-350 parked on the street. Hacking coughs erupted from him, but he was still conscious enough to glare at her. He was doing better than she'd expected. She'd grant him a small smidgen of respect for that. Not that she regretted poisoning him. He shouldn't have come after her.

The platinum blonde girl from before stood right in front of Debbie's door, her hands on her hips, her face contorted in rage.

"You hurt Shorty," the girl barked. "How dare you?"

Debbie sneered. "Scram, tiny meat. I don't want to hurt some kid, but I will if you try to be a big girl and get in my way. Learn from your friend's mistake."

The girl lifted both of her hands and opened her palms. Orbs of purple light sprang into existence. "Well, that's nice. I'm Alison Brownstone, and I don't have any problem hurting someone who hurt my friend."

Debbie gritted her teeth. A witch, or something else? The bounty hunters weren't the only ones who had misjudged their opponent.

The witch charged the girl, hoping to take her off-guard. Alison flicked her wrists with a smirk.

A massive flash blinded Debbie and she stumbled back, her hands shooting to her eyes. She dropped her satchel.

"You little bitch," she hissed. "Do you have any idea who I am? Do you have any idea of my power?" She flailed blindly. "You'll pay for this."

Alison slammed a hard fist into the witch's stomach and followed up with a few quick head-punches.

The witch cried out and dropped to the ground, this time clutching her stomach with one hand and her head with the other. Her eyes were still trying to readjust after the magical flare, but everything remained an indistinct blur.

The girl laughed. "My Aunt Shay taught me that combo. I've been working all summer on strength training, you know. Probably couldn't have taken out Shorty with it, but it worked well enough on you." She leaned closer. "My dad and aunt are always telling me, 'Alison, don't always rely on magic. You never know when it won't work for you.' That's your problem. If you'd hit the gym or taken a few self-defense courses you might not be in this position."

Debbie moaned. "I will fucking kill you. I don't care if you're a Brownstone."

Trey rushed around the corner, a frown on his face, and a gun out. He pointed it at the witch. "Don't even *think* about moving. You owe me a new suit." Crimson stains spread over his white shirt, but he didn't grimace.

Brownstone stepped around the corner, his face locked in a grim frown, and his gun also out.

Two other bounty hunters came running around the

opposite end, guns out. They were also in suits. Were all bounty hunters so fashionable?

Debbie sighed as her vision cleared. She looked at all the men and finally back at the smirking girl. She'd been taken down by some kid. Talk about embarrassing.

"I'll get you someday for this, Alison Brownstone."

The girl rolled her eyes. "I've dealt with much scarier people than you." She nodded toward Brownstone. "My dad, for one."

Trey moved over to Debbie and roughly pulled her hands behind her back. He cuffed her, patted her down, and pulled out all the vials in her pockets.

"Lachlan, Russell, take this bitch to the station." He fished his keys out of his pocket and tossed them to Russell.

"Where you going?" the other bounty hunter asked.

Trey pointed to the hacking Shorty. "We need to get his ass to a hospital. That don't take a whole team, though."

Russell frowned. "You don't look so good yourself."

Trey frowned and looked down at the bloodstains. "Yeah, bulletproof vests ain't shit against shrapnel. Whatever. I'm fine."

Shorty hacked and wheezed again.

"It's okay, brother. We'll get you to a doctor."

Debbie laughed. "Doctor? They won't be able to help him. You shouldn't have come for me. I still win. If you let me go, I'll give you a potion that will counter the effects."

Brownstone stepped forward and shook his head. "Don't worry, Trey. I know someone." He nodded to Trey. "You come with me. Alison, you go with the others, but make sure she's out first. She might have some tricks still up her sleeve. Oh, and don't tell Shay about this shit."

Alison nodded and glared down at Debbie. She knelt by the woman and placed a hand close to her face.

"What are you doing?" Debbie asked.

The girl offered her a cold smile as her hand started glowing. "Just making you a little sleepy. It won't hurt. Unfortunately."

"What the hell are you?" Debbie whispered, then gave in to the darkness.

James frowned as he paced Zoe's living room, his arms crossed.

Fucking sloppy. Too fucking sloppy. Only lucky neither of the guys is dead. I should have ended that bitch, but I couldn't do that in front of Alison.

The potions witch clucked her tongue as she handed a green potion to the coughing and wheezing Shorty. "Drink this."

She also handed a healing potion to Trey.

Both bounty hunters swallowed the potions in one quick gulp. Shorty immediately stopped coughing, and Trey closed his eyes and let out a sigh of relief. It'd been a while since anyone in the Brownstone Agency had come that close to serious injury.

James frowned. He should have just kicked in the door and taken the witch out himself.

"I don't mean to tell you your business, James, but I'm a bit surprised." Zoe arched a brow at him. "You've purchased quite a few potions from me for your team. Why didn't you have one on you? It was a good thing you brought the poisoned man to me since the regular potions wouldn't have worked, but your other man would have been fine with a normal potion, and he wouldn't have had to suffer on his way here."

The bounty hunter grunted. "Didn't have any with us. Weren't expecting a level-two bounty to be a potions witch."

Zoe smirked. "Well, the fact that I was able to help your man there so easily shows she wasn't much of one compared to me. Knowing that really makes my day."

I wonder if I should have used Whispy Doom? Damn it, there was just no way to know a level two was gonna go that way.

James had his amulet with him, not that he wanted to tell Zoe that. Even his men didn't know about it yet.

He'd promised Alison that he would always wear it, even though he only bonded with it in emergencies. Good old Whispy Doom had been getting more and more talkative in his mind. James was no longer disturbed by it, but the damned amulet could be distracting.

It was easier to ignore the amulet when it only managed unintelligible whispers. The bloodthirsty thing seemed obsessed with convincing him to kill every bounty he encountered or foe he battled.

James turned away from Zoe and frowned. Alison had done well, but if he'd known their target was a witch, he wouldn't have risked bringing the girl along. His daughter might be learning at school, and he knew she was capable of more than she'd told him, but having her tag along against a few minor criminals was different than taking on rogue witches or dark wizards.

I should ask her school if they have some sort of magical self-defense class. Don't they have to teach that kind of thing at magic school?

Yeah, fucking father of the year. I only want my daughter around normal-ass criminals.

Trey shook his head and ran his hands over his torn suit. "I've had worse. The real sacrifice here were these fine threads. Got a potion that can fix my suit?" He smirked. "Or would something like that be more expensive than just buying a new suit?"

Zoe tilted her head to offer Trey a seductive smile, her dark hair framing her face. "Sorry, sweetie, but I specialize mostly in living things." She ran a hand over her hip, drawing attention to her tight miniskirt, as she licked her lips. "I wish I could help you. I really do."

James resisted a snort.

I'm too dangerous to hit on, but the guys aren't? Maybe I should have warned them before bringing them here. It's like bringing sheep directly to the wolf.

Trey smirked and adjusted his tie. He clearly liked what he saw in the witch.

James cleared his throat. He wasn't there to hook Zoe and Trey up.

Shorty took a few deep breaths. His coughing had completely subsided. "That was some bullshit, yo. I thought we was gonna walk into an easy level two, not get all mustard gas shit in my face like it's the fucking Battle of Ypres."

James had no clue what had happened at the Battle of

Ypres. Half the time anymore, the guys used military references he couldn't follow. Military history rarely intersected with barbeque.

Royce is turning them more into Marines than bounty hunters.

Trey frowned. "We fucked up. We didn't have enough intel. We shouldn't assume so much, or just think the only thing we need to worry about is what's written in the bounty reports." He shrugged. "We forgot our Sun Tzu."

No, not Marines, ancient Chinese generals.

"If you know the enemy and know yourself, you need not fear the result of a hundred battles," Trey and Shorty recited in unison. "If you know yourself but not the enemy, for every victory gained, you will also suffer a defeat."

Zoe blinked and looked at James. He shrugged.

The historical wisdom crap was Staff Sergeant Royce's thing, not his, but the guys got something out of it, so he wasn't going to complain. The important thing was everyone agreed the bounty confrontation shouldn't have gone down like it did. They'd fucked up.

"Any bounty can be a surprise," James observed. "The more you know, the fewer people get hurt." He shrugged. "But even I didn't think some level two would know magic. You're right, though. We've been focusing the guys so much on captures that maybe we've let the information-gathering shit get a little weak, and that could get someone killed. We need to fucking do better."

Zoe let out a soft laugh. "You're all far too young to be so old-fashioned."

James frowned. "What do you mean?"

She shrugged and sauntered into her kitchen. "Tea?"

The men all shook their heads.

"I'm just saying, it's not like the return of magic happened yesterday. It's been decades now. There are wizard kiddies everywhere now, and it's only going to get worse." She poured herself some tea from a pitcher sitting next to her sink. A large orange and yellow plant twitched and shuddered beside it. "You need to up your game, guys."

2

A couple of days later, James' F-350 rumbled down the road with him, Shay, and Alison inside. The girl's single suitcase sat beside her in the back seat.

Shit. I knew it was coming, but it's still hard to believe summer vacation is already over.

"Just so you know, Alison," James began, "I've been putting your share of the bounties into your account. Between the money from the sale of your house and the money you made this summer, when you graduate you shouldn't have any money troubles at all."

She laughed. "I'm graduating from magic school. It's not like I think I'm going to have a lot of problems."

James shrugged. "Maybe. Money's a magic all its own."

Shay snorted. "Ain't *that* the truth."

The bounty hunter spared her a glance. Considering how much money she'd earned on some of her tomb raids, she might have more money stashed away than him. It was hard to say, given all her fancy warehouses and trips around the world. A complicated lifestyle ended up expensive.

"Guess I'll be a spoiled little rich girl." Alison smiled. "Still, thank you, Dad. You could have kept the money from my house. You didn't have to do all this training or give me any more money."

"You earned that money," he rumbled. "Especially on that last bounty. She might have gotten away if you hadn't used your magic."

"I'm just saying. I love talking to you on the phone, but it's only when I'm back that I remember why I love being Alison Brownstone so much." She shrugged and quieted.

Fuck. I should say something. She's pouring her heart out here.

James managed a grunt in response.

Maybe it was stupid to worry about Alison having money when both Shay and James were rich by any normal standard, but if there were one thing he could give his daughter, it would be independence. The priests who had helped raise him had done that for him, and he only hoped he could do as well by Alison. If he managed only that, he would consider himself a halfway-decent father.

The silence stretched. It was not an awkward lack of conversation, but more a mutual understanding and respect among everyone in the car. He'd half-expected Alison to resent being taken away from the magic school and having to deal with the dark, dirty reality that was Los Angeles, but the summer had been a good experience for everyone. Far better than James could have ever anticipated.

Sure, he'd had to go to court to keep her. Plus, he'd had

to beat down a Drow queen, but some problems just came with being James Brownstone.

He changed lanes and cleared his throat. "Still don't know if I like you doing this magic train crap instead of taking a plane back. Sounds complicated."

Alison shrugged. "It's not a big deal. It's way simpler than flying back. You're the one so obsessed with things being safe for me, and the train is much safer than me taking a flight back. Non-magical people can't even get on these trains, so that's…what, most of the people on the planet who can't attack me on the way back to school?"

James wanted to argue more but shut his mouth. Alison being independent meant taking advantage of the things that played to her strengths. Just because he didn't find magic simple and distrusted it didn't mean she did, even if he still didn't trust some hidden magical underground train.

He turned into a Starbucks parking lot. "I always wondered why there were so many of these places."

Shay smirked. "People can't just like coffee?"

James shrugged. "Just saying that every time I think about it, I wonder about a lot of stuff. Like if McDonald's is secretly some magical dragon parking place."

He looked at Alison, and she shrugged.

The bounty hunter stepped out of the truck and headed to the back to pull out Alison's suitcase. She hopped out of her seat without trouble. It was times like this he almost forgot she was blind.

Alison ran over to him and pulled him into a hug. "This has been a great summer, Dad. You taught me a lot, and I truly became Alison Brownstone."

He ruffled her hair. "I didn't need some court to tell me that you're my daughter."

The girl pulled away and wiped the tears out of her eyes. "Promise me you'll always wear your amulet when I'm gone." She pointed at his chest. "No matter if you think it's the easiest job in the world. I don't want to have to worry about you. If a level two can end up a witch, a level four might really be a six."

James sighed. "I promise."

Alison took the handle of her suitcase and waved goodbye to both of them. James stood there in the parking lot as the girl entered the Starbucks and headed toward the bathroom.

Why do they to walk toward the bathroom to get to the magic train? Magic. Always so fucking weird.

Not that he had much a right to talk. James patted the amulet resting underneath his shirt.

Not sure if this is magic or something else, but Whispy Doom is weird.

Maria sipped her coffee, then frowned, eyeing the cup. No one liked lukewarm coffee.

"Damn it, Weber," Maria muttered to herself. "Can't you get me a halfway decent cup of coffee? It's already late. How the hell am I supposed to not fall asleep after being here for twelve hours?"

She set the cup down and continued scrolling through the Homeland Security Daily Enhanced Threat Bulletin. Despite all the technology and magic the government had access to, high-level bounties still managed to wander the country freely.

Well, Los Angeles is my problem, so I'll just worry about that.

The lieutenant kept scrolling and clicking, checking the reported movements of every level five and six bounty in the country. After several more minutes of checking, she chuckled.

Nobody even looks like they're coming this way. We've got tens of millions of people, but no high-level bounty wants to come try their luck? Since when did they all become such pussies?

Not all that long ago, the AET lieutenant might have attributed the lack of major threats to luck or the efficiency of the LAPD AET.

True, they'd taken out their share of level fives in the last year, including several Drow and Tessa Vansant, but Maria had no illusions about the actual reason high-level bounties were avoiding LA.

James Brownstone. Scourge of Harriken. Granite Gargoyle. A man who'd taken down more high-level bounties than any other bounty hunter in the country, possibly the world.

Every news story about him was followed by fewer higher-level bounties showing up. The low-level cockroaches must have believed he wouldn't bother with them, but now he had his agency to fumigate them.

As much as it pained Maria to admit, his little pay-per-view stunt with Tyler had only made the fear among the underworld more obvious. She tracked the high-level bounty rumors daily, and after his little bout that some were calling the "Hail to the King" smackdown, several known high-level criminals suddenly seemed far more interested in going to cities other than LA.

It's like having our own personal nuclear weapon that everyone's afraid of.

Maria grinned and picked up the coffee cup. She'd only taken half a sip before remembering its temperature. She rolled her eyes and set it down.

She clicked off the Homeland Security bulletin. There still seemed to be a few level fours, but she was far less concerned with them.

"Might as well see what's going on in the rest of world," Maria mumbled as she switched to her email. Her eyes narrowed. "You've got to be fucking kidding me."

Thirty minutes later, the lieutenant sat at the head of a long table in a conference room, the key members of the AET team lining the table. She resisted the urge to chew Weber out about the coffee.

Maria cleared her throat. "I've just been informed that the Los Angeles Museum of Natural History will tomorrow be opening a display of Oriceran magical artifacts as part of a short-term exhibit, but for some reason that escapes me, the museum hasn't requested additional protection for the artifacts. Since these are on loan from the Light Elves, I'm surprised that their people at the consulate haven't asked for protection."

It wasn't lost on her that neither she nor her men had realized this major exhibit was going to open. The LAPD

AET weren't the most cultured group of men and women, apparently.

Sergeant Weber furrowed his brow. "You think someone's going to target the artifacts?"

"Damn right, I do. It's just too tempting. These things aren't just valuable but are actual magic items. Anyone who gets their hands on them gets a big payday, or potentially becomes the newest weirdo we have to worry about on the daily enhanced threat briefing."

Matthews frowned from the other end of the table. "So? If museum people think they've got it, they probably do. Probably hired a bunch of fancy magical private security, or maybe got some people from the consulate to help guard it. If they didn't ask it's not our problem, and I don't see why we should have to risk our lives over it."

Several others nodded their agreement. Their heads snapped toward Maria when she slammed her fist on the table.

"*Not our problem*? We're the police. Have some fucking pride in your uniform. If random assholes come into our town and commit a high-profile artifact theft right underneath our noses, we'll be laughingstocks. Not to mention, if said assholes get their hands on a bunch of magical artifacts, who knows what kind of bullshit they might be able to pull off?"

The men all looked down.

"What about Brownstone?" Weber asked. "I mean, we could just happen to mention to him that someone's coming into town to stir up trouble."

Maria shook her head. "He's a bounty hunter, not a

security guard. If we don't have someone specific to point him at, he's not going to be a help."

"So what's the play, then?"

She frowned. "I'll contact the museum later and see what help they need. Once we know that, we can better figure out how to deploy our resources."

James sat on Shay's couch trying to fight off the melancholy that wanted to settle over him. He'd gotten used to Alison being at school last semester, but having her over the summer now made for a painful separation. Much more than he'd ever expected.

Guess this is part of what it means to be a parent, too.

He grunted and shook his head.

Shay let out a quiet chuckle. "It's all right if you'll miss her, you know. You're her dad now, so you're supposed to care about her."

"I figured it'd take a little longer before I missed her."

She sighed and leaned her head back. "It's definitely going to be less fun here. I was having a good time training Alison."

"You still have Lily, at least."

"Yeah, I do." Shay shook her head. "But it's not the same." She chuckled.

"What's so funny?"

Shay shrugged. "We talked about it the other day during your little rooftop romantic dessert deal."

James grunted. He still wasn't sure if he'd pulled the surprise off well. She'd seemed to like it, and he'd done everything the podcasts had told him to, but hearing her bare her soul that night had unsettled him more than he'd expected.

Shit. Usually, when I don't know how to deal with someone's emotions I ask Shay, but it's not like I can ask her how to deal with her. Can I?

Shay is just as confused as I am about a lot of this shit. Don't know if that makes me feel better or worse.

The woman stared at him, her lips pursed.

Shit. Is she pissed because I'm not saying anything? What should I do? What would the podcasts say? Maybe I should call Alison and ask.

A man needed to know his weaknesses. Words weren't his strength. It was time for action.

James reached over and pulled Shay into a tight hug. She frowned for a few moments and punched him lightly before relaxing and hugging him back.

After a moment, she patted him on the arm. "I'm tapping out! Can't breathe, you mountain of muscle."

He jerked back, his eyes widening. "You okay?"

Shay laughed. "All this time together, and you still can't tell when I'm joking?" She winked and stood. "Come with me. I've got something to show you."

James followed with a slight frown. Had he screwed up? Was he about to be punished?

The tomb raider led him to her bedroom. Maybe he was being rewarded. He allowed himself a little grin at the thought.

Once inside the bedroom, Shay pointed toward the bathroom. "I've been selfish."

She entered the bathroom and grabbed a toothbrush

holder and an unopened toothbrush. She handed them to James.

His gaze flicked between the bathroom and the bed. Maybe she wanted to take a shower together, but he couldn't figure out how the toothbrush fit in.

Maybe Shay's kinkier than I thought.

"Selfish?" he asked. Sometimes not asking too many questions was the best way to avoid looking like a dumbass.

"Yes. I've got my own little space at your house, but I won't even let you have a side of the sink at mine. If we're going to be together, I need to stop acting like I will run off at any second. Not ready to move in with you, but this is kind of a nice compromise." She rubbed the back of her neck. "So, fair is fair. Why don't you take the left side of my bathroom?"

James nodded slowly. The rooftop confession had been a big deal, but those were just words in the end. This meant something more.

Shay pulled her shirt over her head. "After you take care of that, we can have a little fun."

The bounty hunter marched over to her dresser to set down the toothbrush and holder before turning back to soak in his girlfriend stripping.

Hey, that's some new and pretty lacy underwear.

She smirked. "You couldn't get to the bathroom before your mind was on me, huh? Maybe you *are* a keeper, James Brownstone."

3

Maria drummed her fingers against her desk as she waited on hold. There had been two transfers already during her call to the museum, and she was on this hold for over five agonizing minutes.

It's not like I'm some random idiot calling. I'm a damned LAPD AET lieutenant. You think they would be a little more accommodating.

Now she was stuck listening to light classical music and waiting for someone to start acting like a call from the LAPD was halfway important.

"Lieutenant Hall?" came a voice over the line.

Maria sat up. "Yes. To whom I am speaking?"

"I'm Spencer Preston, I'm Head of Security for the museum."

The lieutenant let out a sigh of relief. "Ah, finally. They kept bouncing me around to a bunch of people who didn't know what is going on."

"I apologize for the inconvenience, Lieutenant. We

---

strive to maintain a good relationship with the local authorities."

"Of course." The lieutenant rubbed the back of her neck. "I was a bit surprised, though, that the museum didn't put in a formal request for police protection during your exhibit. I thought maybe you just hadn't known to request AET protection so I hadn't seen it, but when I checked with the other departments, no one has any record of you requesting police aid."

Spencer let out a quiet chuckle. "Why would I do that?"

"Excuse me?"

"Why would we request police protection?"

Maria blinked. "Okay, let me verify some facts before we continue this conversation."

"Of course."

"Is the museum now hosting an exhibit of rare Oriceran magical artifacts?"

Spencer cleared his throat. "Yes, that's accurate. You're quite welcome to come over and view the exhibit."

"And these are active magical artifacts? Not just some old crown that used to have power?"

"Oh. I see." The man laughed. "You're worried that we've been duped about the provenance of the objects. I can understand that concern. Anyone in the business of artifacts these days has to deal with so many disreputable people and be cautious, but I can assure you, Lieutenant, that not only do we have all the necessary paperwork, but we've also had each artifact verified by third parties well-versed in the magical arts. There's no fraud here, and thus no need for the police."

Is this guy purposely trying to annoy me, or is he really that thick?

Maria pinched the bridge of her nose. "You're not understanding what I'm getting at. I'm with LAPD AET. We field teams to deal with magical threats beyond the capabilities of normal officers or even SWAT."

"I must say, then, that I'm even more confused now. Oh." His snap was audible even over the phone. "You're worried these artifacts will explode or leak magic or something like that." Another laugh came, the mocking tone obvious. "It's nothing like that. I can assure you. We have all the necessary paperwork with the government and have verified the general display safety of these objects. The only injuries we have to worry about are from people standing too long."

Maria wanted to bang her head against her desk but sighed instead.

"No, no. Mr. Preston, what I'm worried about is pretty straightforward. You have a bunch of valuable magical artifacts, and I'm concerned that an enhanced threat, Oriceran or otherwise, will blow a hole in the side of your museum and steal all those fancy magical artifacts. That's why I was surprised you're not requesting police protection. I'm worried you don't understand the risks."

Spencer sniffed disdainfully. "We understand the risks. It's not exactly like this museum has never handled an artifact before, Miss Hall."

Miss Hall? Oh, no you didn't.

Maria waited a few seconds, wondering if she should remind him that she was Lieutenant Hall, but decided against it.

"From what I've read," she offered instead, "this is the largest collection of artifacts you've ever handled. I think it represents a unique danger and temptation for criminals."

"I can assure you that we have and will take all necessary precautions. We do not require police protection, and, not to be rude, we can't risk untrained personnel bumbling around our expensive items. Thank you for your concern, Miss Hall, but I'm very busy, and I can't spend any more time discussing this with you. If you want to make an appointment, please contact museum reception."

"We're not done—"

The call ended.

Maria held her phone away from her face and stared at it. The sonofabitch'd had the nerve to hang up on her.

She took a few deep breaths and placed her phone on her desk. Spencer Preston obviously thought they wouldn't have any trouble, but she found it hard to believe that if a level-five criminal attacked the museum they were equipped to fend him off.

No. The lieutenant wasn't about to take some stuffed shirt's word for it. She was going to stop by and see for herself just how good their security was.

James' eyes flicked open, and he yawned. Exhausted, too damned exhausted. He wasn't even sure why he was so tired.

Guess without Alison around, I feel a little older and more tired. Weird to wake up and know I won't be having breakfast with her.

He rose and grabbed his clothes. The smooth metal of the separator skimmed his chest. He looked down at the amulet connected to it.

Wonder if he has to sleep? If I kept him bonded to me at all times, would he get tired? Would I?

James shook his head. He still had far too many questions and not enough answers about the amulet.

Shay's recent revelation that other aliens had visited Earth, and that they might even be from his home planet, complicated things. It wasn't like finding out that he was actually an alien who'd probably had his DNA altered by a strange amulet fit in all that well with his desire for a simple life.

Not only that, the more he learned about the amulet, the less convinced he was that its creators had been a benevolent species.

I used to think this thing might be demonic, but you can be a total fucker even without being a demon.

According to Shay, the government was tracking alien artifacts and other evidence of non-Oriceran intelligent species through Project Ragnarok and Project Nephilim.

That meant James had to be careful not to reveal to anyone he didn't trust the true nature of the artifact, but so far, only Peyton and Shay knew the truth.

I still should be experimenting with it more. It gave me that weird vision change during the shit with Lars. That means it can do a lot more than I've ever realized. This shit might be the key to dealing with real nasty assholes in the future.

He moved over to the dresser to grab the toothbrush holder and toothbrush. They were gone, and a quick survey of the bedroom didn't reveal them.

It wasn't like toiletries got up and wandered off on their own. Or did they?

Shit. I hope Shay didn't give me a living toothbrush and toothbrush holder. Dealing with Whispy Doom is bad enough. I don't want to have a conversation with my toothbrush every day.

James stopped and grunted. He'd finally spotted the errant toothbrush and holder. They sat on the left side of the sink in the bathroom.

It was time for a little hygiene.

A few minutes later, James made his way down the stairs in his jeans but not his shirt. Shay sat at the dining room table, a paper cup of coffee in hand and large white paper bag sitting on the table.

"A lot of breakfast sandwiches," she explained. "I might not make breakfast very well, but I can order it and pick it up with the best of 'em." She smiled and nodded toward the bag. "And you're a man of…extreme appetites, so I bought a lot." Her eyebrows lifted suggestively.

James gave a nod and plopped himself into a chair. He pulled out a sausage biscuit and downed the thing in two bites.

A satisfied smirk settled over Shay's face. "Looks like I made the right choice." She took another sip of her coffee. "It's been a hard summer."

James swallowed. "Hard? How so?

She laughed. "You almost got yourself killed, for one."

"That's kind of an every-week thing for me."

"Okay, good point." Shay shook her finger. "Still, you

had the custody battle to worry about, along with the media circus, not to mention trying to teach Alison as much as you could." She shrugged. "Dealing with all that is, well, more complicated than the typical ass-kicking you do.

"I didn't think of it that way, but I guess you're right." This time he dug out a bacon and egg biscuit.

Shay offered James a soft smile. "And now she's back in school, and I know you're gonna have trouble with missing her."

"There'll be parents' weekends."

"Sure, but seeing her every few months isn't the same thing as seeing her every day, and you know it."

James grunted and shrugged. "It's what's best for her, and I can put on my big-boy pants and just deal with it." He put down his sandwich. "What about you? You flying off somewhere soon? Some weird-ass secret country I've never heard of?"

Shay shook her head. "Nah, I figured I should take a couple of weeks off because someone might need me."

"Huh? Who?"

She rolled her eyes. "It's always two steps forward, one step back with you. *You* need me, James. I think you'll be more depressed than you realize without Alison, so I'm gonna stick around and cheer you up. When you're busy, I'll train and keep an eye out for jobs, and unless something fucking fantastic comes up, I'll stay in town."

James frowned. "There *is* something you can help me with."

She smirked. "You need to give me a day between bedroom fun-time sessions. I get sore otherwise."

He shook his head. "Not that. Something else, especially since you have more contacts in the magical world. I've got Zoe, but not much else."

"Since when do you want to use more magic?" Shay narrowed her eyes.

"That job I took Alison on the other day was a cluster-fuck. The level two turned out to be a witch." James frowned at his sandwich as if it were to blame. "Because Alison was there and could pull her magic it ended quickly, and I was about to end it myself, but most times, my guys aren't gonna have a half-Drow princess with them, or me, for that matter. We got caught with our pants down, and next time someone might end up dead." He looked at Shay. "I was hoping you could do some research and find some options. I know the police use those anti-magic deflectors, but it might be hard to get my hands on a lot of those."

Shay ran her finger over the rim of her cup. "Okay, I'll check into that. Just one quick little thing I have to do first."

"What?"

"A bunch of artifacts just came in for a temporary exhibit at the Los Angeles Museum of Natural History. I want to go to the museum to learn more about the pieces."

James chuckled. "Are you gonna become a museum raider?"

Shay shook her head. "Just curious more than anything. It's good to know what's floating around out there in case it ever leaves legal hands."

"I can't come with you. I've got to help in the tactical room. I want the guys to start training for magical confrontations."

"How are you gonna do that?"

James grinned. "I bought a few things from Zoe, and the Professor gave me some shit he had lying around."

"'Shit he had lying around?'" Shay raised an eyebrow.

The bounty hunter shrugged. "That was what he said."

"Okay, just don't blow up your building."

James pushed into the lobby of Camp Brownstone with a box in his arms. He gave a quick nod to Charlyce, who was on the phone. She gave him a smile and a wave, and he continued down the hallway toward the tactical room.

All the available men had gathered. Several of them would be leaving for Vegas the following day to relieve the currently deployed Vegas team.

Half the men were already in their tactical jumpsuits, and the others were still pulling theirs on.

Trey grinned from the wall in the corner of the room. "It's the big man himself. I was starting to think you were too chickenshit to show up."

James grunted. "Afraid of you guys? You'll have to do a shitload more training before you can take me down, especially if I'm not by myself." He set down the box and pulled off his boots, then went over to a locker to pull out one of the larger tactical suits. "Before we start all this shit, I wanted to remind you all about the barbeque class on Saturday."

A few people grumbled but shut their mouths when Trey and Shorty gave them death glares.

"Get the fuck out of here with your bitching," Shorty

snarled. "Complaining about the big man taking his own time to teach you! Ingrates."

James shrugged. "Most of the shit we make you do, you only appreciate when you're on the job. At least this way, you'll be able to eat your practice."

"I hear that." Isaiah patted his belly.

Everyone laughed.

The training under Staff Sergeant Royce had melted most of his fat away, but Isaiah would never be the kind of man that anyone would describe as cut.

"It's only for a couple of hours," James explained. "The focus is gonna be on the good use of wood and temperature control. Not gonna tell you that you have to read shit beforehand, but get on the fucking internet and read some shit."

The men all laughed.

James grinned and finished zipping up his suit. He pulled a tactical harness out of the box and strapped it over the jumpsuit, and then began filling his pockets and pouches with vials containing potions and several colors of small glass figurines.

"Royce and I are still figuring out how we can change the tactical room system to simulate magic, but for today, we're gonna do the best thing you can do for training."

"What's that?" Lachlan pulled a rifle simulator from the new metal rack they'd just installed along the wall.

"Royce told me how effective live-fire training can be for Marines," James offered. He held up one of the vials. "So it's time for some live magic training. This is an actual potion."

Shorty groaned. "You gonna fucking poison me, big man?"

"Nothing worse than a little tear gas, from what Zoe told me." James fished out one of the figurines. "I don't know exactly how, but another friend of mine told me this should trip the electronics in your suits, so it's gonna be like getting hit by lightning. Got a few little flashbang figurines, too. The teams are gonna be unbalanced, more of you on one team, then a smaller team with me playing the part of an angry fucking wizard."

Now everyone groaned.

Trey pushed off the wall. "What about taking you out? Even if we hit you, you could probably just use your barbeque blood power to ignore the electrical shocks. If you're throwing this magic shit instead of using your fake rifle, the system won't be able to stop you from keeping coming at us."

James nodded. Even without the amulet the suit probably couldn't take him down, but at least it'd let him know when he got hit.

I wonder if I should use the amulet and see how many hits it would take me to go down? Nah.

"Fair enough. Here's what I'll say: you get three hits on me. Lots of magic assholes have defensive magic, so you should get used to it taking more firepower. I'll shout out each hit, and once you get three, I'm dead."

4

The shrieks and curses of men filled the air in the darkened and smoke-filled tactical room. The occasional flash brightened the room, followed by a loud recorded, but still convincing, peal of thunder. James half-wondered how much it'd cost to install a system to simulate an earthquake. They *were* in California, after all.

James flattened himself near a wall. Half his team, the red team, had already been picked off, the other team apparently hoping to isolate and finish him.

Good strategy. Glad the guys realized you can't just ignore everybody but the main threat.

He pulled out a figurine and spun around the corner to throw it at two men on the blue team. They fired a few rounds and his suit buzzed, indicating they'd come close, but he wasn't shocked.

The figurine collided with a man, and a mass of arcing blue-white energy exploded. Both bounty hunters collapsed to the ground, yowling and twitching as their suits shocked them.

James grinned. So far, no one had managed to get a single hit on him.

Two more of his men got taken out, leaving only James, Manuel, and TJ as the living red team members.

If I can kill a house full of Harriken without my amulet, I can take down my guys in this smoky little room.

Shorty vaulted over a wall and fired. "Die, you wizard motherfucker!"

James gritted his teeth as the suit shocked him. "One hit."

The junior hunter's face split in a huge grin. "Yeah! I did it."

James rushed forward and yanked Shorty's rifle simulator out of his hand and aimed it at him. "You should have kept firing."

"Well, shit, that ain't fair."

"Never drop your weapon, and don't celebrate until the other guy's down." James pulled the trigger and the other bounty hunter fell to the ground, twitching and wincing. He tossed the rifle simulator to the ground.

He jogged toward a corner where several blocks provided cover, his jaw tight. His refusal to drop after being hit resulted in the suit continuing to shock him. The pain might not be enough to take him down, but it wasn't easy to ignore either.

James crouched and grabbed a smoke potion. He uncorked it and chucked it across the room as a distraction. Thick smoke billowed from the bottle, and several blue team members rushed that way and started firing aimlessly, convinced of an incursion.

He sucked in a breath, trying to ignore his muscles'

twitching between the shocks. Until he dropped, they wouldn't stop.

Good way to simulate bleeding out, I guess. I'm wounded, but I can keep going. Just like in a real fight.

James stopped as he spotted the tip of a rifle simulator pointed around a corner on the ground.

Lying down in here is a dumbass move.

After ducking quickly behind a wall, he pulled out another figurine. He'd been doing his best to pace himself so he'd have enough magic toys for the second round, but he'd already used too many. He would figure out what he was going to do about that later.

He peeked around the corner and threw the figurine near the wall right next to the hidden rifle. Averting his eyes from the flash, he rushed forward, ready to strip the blinded man of his weapon and kill him with it.

The bounty hunter cleared the corner and prepared to lay out the wannabe sniper with a mild punch or kick.

What the fuck?

The rifle lay on the ground, propped against the wall. No one was behind it. A disabled Lachlan lay several yards away with a grin on his face. The only thing James didn't get was how his rifle had ended up in such a conspicuous spot. If he'd moved more than a few inches, the suit would have shocked him.

Shit. That means...

James spun.

"Surprise, motherfucker," shouted Trey from behind him.

The grinning ambusher fired at point blank range into

James' chest and then his head. The quick shocks jolted James, but he didn't fall.

"Two," he shouted. "And three hits." He lowered himself to the ground and lay down. The shocks ceased. "Guess I'm fucking dead. Not as bad as I thought it'd be."

Trey smirked and shrugged. "Got too cocky, big man."

James grunted. "You're right. Good job. I don't rely much on fancy tactics and tricks on jobs, but it'll help even the playing field for you when you run into high-level threats." He grunted. "But next time, shoot first, then taunt. With magical assholes, you might only get one shot."

The other man snorted. "Shoot first? That ain't no fun."

Fifteen minutes into the second round with switched teams, the battle wasn't going as well for Team Brownstone. James had been forced to be less aggressive. He wondered if every hint of movement he saw was a trap, just like the two shadows he saw on the back wall.

He pulled out the last magical item he had, a small figurine—one of his so-called lightning simulators—and threw it against the wall. Blue-white arcs of energy shot from the source of impact and two screams echoed in the room.

James frowned. He considered rushing over to grab a rifle simulator but decided he had a better idea. It was important for the men to not just focus on firearms or flashy magic, but the very real threat that could come up close.

"Take that, motherfuckers," Trey shouted from the second level.

Glad he's on my team this round.

Trey blazed away at a group of pinned enemies trying to make their way up the ramp to take out Shorty and him.

James took the opportunity to jog down the opposite side. He stopped and stepped into an alcove, his large frame barely fitting, and waited with his back against the wall.

It was right there in the name: bounty *hunter*. Hunters required patience.

Manuel crept around the corner and spotted James, hesitating for a moment, likely because he'd been on the other man's team not all that long before. A mistake.

James ripped the rifle simulator out of his hand and yanked the man forward. He spun Manuel around and slapped his meaty arm around the man's neck, and his chokehold had the other man unconscious in seconds. He let him fall to the ground.

"Yo, Manuel, what do you see?" TJ called from around the corner.

They've gotten too used to hearing people scream or yell or even tell jokes once they're on the ground. Don't even always have screams in a real fight, especially when you've split up.

James crept toward TJ but kept his back to the wall.

"This ain't funny, man," TJ called. "What's going on? We're getting creamed over on the other side."

Three...two...one.

James rushed around the corner and bowled into the very surprised TJ. The junior bounty hunter's weapon flew out of his hand and skidded across the floor. He watched James, wide-eyed, clearly not sure what he should do.

Seconds later, he lay on the ground unconscious just like Manuel, the victim of another chokehold.

His attacker picked up TJ's weapon and strode toward the ramp, where the men were still exchanging fire with the upper-level defenders.

"Got to watch your sides," James rumbled. He whipped up the rifle simulator and opened fire.

Half the men turned to fire at him. The other half ran up the ramp.

James winced as electricity jolted through him and winced again at another blast of energy.

"Two hits," James shouted and continued firing.

The crossfire had the other side on the ground within fifteen seconds, twitching in pain.

"That's all of them, big man," Trey shouted with a grin. He glanced to the side and frowned. "What the fuck happened to Manuel and TJ?"

James shrugged. "I helped them take a little nap."

Maria stepped into the main entrance of the museum. No uniform, just casual wear. Four armed guards in red uniforms stood in the lobby, all with Tasers and pistols and crystal necklaces around their necks. Anti-magic deflectors, most likely.

Something about them seemed off, though, but she'd only ever seen a few designs, so it wasn't like she could claim extensive expertise.

Maybe they are something else.

After buying her ticket, she made her way down the

hallway toward the Treasures of Oriceran Exhibit. Two more armed guards stood at a checkpoint with a table and a metal detector.

Good thing I didn't bring my gun.

Maria queued behind several other people and waited as they were waved through. She stepped through the metal detector, but one of the guards held up his hand after she stepped out.

"I'm sorry for the inconvenience, ma'am, but you've been selected for further security inspection." He nodded toward a folding metal chair in front of the table. "Please sit there."

She thought about protesting, but the line of impatient visitors combined with the four different cameras in the hallway convinced her it would be a bad idea. Instead, she moved to the chair, sat, and crossed her arms.

"What's this about?" she asked the guard behind the table.

"This won't take long." He held up a clear glass orb. "Please extend your palm."

"What's this?" Maria frowned.

Talk about extensive security. If she weren't mistaken, the orb was some sort of truth detection artifact.

"It's just a kind of danger sensor," the guard explained. "Don't worry. It won't hurt, but I'm afraid you can't proceed any farther without this test."

She rolled her eyes and extended her palm. "Whatever."

The man set the orb in her palm. "Do you have any intention of damaging or stealing the artifacts in the exhibit, ma'am?"

"What the hell?" She narrowed her eyes. "No."

He watched the orb for several seconds, his hand on the grip of his gun.

Touchy.

The orb didn't change, and the man smiled. "I apologize for the inconvenience. You're free to go, ma'am."

Maria tossed the orb back to him and stood with a snort. She made her way down the hall into another room with multiple guards wearing anti-magic deflectors. One of the guards had a holstered wand.

A dozen cordoned-off display cases stood around the room, each containing a different artifact. A small plaque stood next to each, along with a button to activate the holographic guide.

The lieutenant looked up and around. No large vents. No windows. There was no other door from what she could see, either.

Maria walked over to the nearest artifact. She wasn't an expert on alarm systems, but even she could spot the small strip around the display cases. An electronic fence, probably laser or infrared.

She leaned toward the case, which contained a simple silver circlet. According to the plaque, it was the Circlet of the Lost Gnome King. She pressed the button.

A translucent hologram of a smiling young woman appeared. "So many years of civilization combined with the myriad of sentient beings on Oriceran has rendered their history uniquely complex. This is even more true in the case of the alleged Lost Gnome King.

"Some claim this legendary king ruled over a large number of gnomes prior to the Great War, but that as a result of dark Atlantean magic, the memory of this gnome kingdom was completely wiped out. Currently, other than a few cryptic notes on a figurine recovered from an area mostly destroyed in the war, there's no actual evidence that this Lost Gnome King ever existed, leading some to suggest he was merely a symbol of gnomic resistance during the war.

"None of the living gnomes, including those who lived through the war, report dealing with this particular gnome king, but oddly enough, some of the older gnomes have also not denied that he might exist. In addition, Oriceran scholars have verified that the circlet possesses magic related to memory manipulation. Please press the button again within ten seconds if you want to hear more."

Maria shook her head and walked toward the next case. The story she'd just heard was the kind of thing that made her wish the Oricerans had stayed on their own planet. The mere fact they could find people to ask about something that had happened thousands of years ago made her head hurt.

How can we hope to keep up with these guys? If they were serious, they could probably conquer Earth. What good are nukes and missiles against teleporters and mind-wipers?

The next artifact looked like a simple wooden bowl. Maria was just about to lean in to read the plaque when she jerked back and blinked.

Shay Carson was reading the plaque, her finger to her lip, her back to the lieutenant.

"You're about the last person I expected to see here," Maria muttered. "I really hope you're not here to do something we'll both regret."

Still looking forward, the other woman shook her head.

"If I were, Lieutenant, you wouldn't have seen me, now would you?" Shay turned around and grinned. "And why can't I come to the museum?"

"I don't know." The cop shrugged. "Let's just say your boyfriend doesn't seem like the museum-going type."

Shay laughed. "Yeah, you've got me there. This would bore James to tears unless it was about Oriceran barbeque equipment." She shrugged. "But I'm a little different. You haven't checked into me at all?"

"A little. I kind of figure sometimes ignorance is bliss."

"I lecture at UCLA on revised history and archaeology. History's always been a passion of mine." Shay shrugged.

"That shit's real?"

"What, UCLA?"

Maria rolled her eyes. "I mean, I didn't actually think you taught." She eyed the woman like she was a bear who had just recited a sonnet. "Seriously?"

"Seriously." Shay pointed to the bowl. "Bowl of the Winds. That thing, in powerful enough hands, could probably make a tornado."

"Shit. We're letting them show magical WMDs?"

Shay shook her head. "Nah. Here's the funny part… It's almost never been used that way, and it's actually rather hard to pull off without a lot of specialized power and knowledge. Basically, you'd probably have to be powerful enough to do it without using the bowl."

Maria nodded. "What's it actually for?"

"It was created by an elven prince who wanted to make sure his wife always had a breeze for her garden. Interesting, huh?" Shay pointed to the first display. "I saw you looking at the Circlet of the Lost Gnome King."

Maria shook her head. "Do you believe all that crap about some guy having a kingdom that nobody remembers now?"

"Sure. Given what's happened with Earth history, I'm not even remotely surprised that they occasionally screwed up theirs as well." Shay grinned. "That's what makes history so exciting right now. We're still digging into the truth." She glanced down at her watch. "I was going to go grab a bite to eat. Want to join me? Your entrance ticket is good until the end of the day."

The cop gave one final glance around at the room. "Sure. I could get something."

Maria took another bite of her pasta as the other woman worked on a slice of pepperoni pizza.

Shay frowned and shook her head. "You know what the problem with having a practically live-in pizza chef is?"

"Huh? No." Maria shrugged.

"It spoils you." Shay sighed and set the pizza back on her plate. "This just isn't very good."

"Brownstone's into pizza and barbeque?"

Shay shook her head. "I'd love it if I could get James to start obsessing over pizza. Every time I talk to him about it, he blows me off by saying he still has to master barbeque. No, just a co-worker of mine who is good with pizza."

"A co-worker?" Maria laughed. "I don't even want to know."

MICHAEL ANDERLE

Shay folded her hands in front of her. "So what was the real reason you were at the museum?"

"What, a cop can't be interested in history?"

"Sure they can, but I love history, and I lecture to people who love history, and I do jobs related to history. You don't have the eyes of someone who loves history. You have the eyes of a cop who is looking for trouble."

Maria shrugged. "Okay, I'll admit I was there to check out their security."

"Why? Someone targeting them?"

The cop considered lying for a moment. She shook her head. "No known threats, but ten-thousand-year-old crowns and tornado bowls, or any of the other stuff in there, is the kind of thing I imagine people want to steal. I contacted the museum the other day about police assistance, and those assholes all but laughed me off." She gritted her teeth and sighed. "I've got to admit, I'm annoyed. The security is nice. Not that I wanted them to have shit security, but I wanted to take the sanctimonious asshole head of security down a few pegs."

Shay snickered. "Maybe your wish can still come true, Lieutenant."

"What do you mean?"

"Their security *was* shit. Massive holes."

Maria frowned. "Armed guards with anti-magic deflectors all over the place. Cameras. That metal detector. Only one major entrance."

Shay shook her head. "The bulk of their network is in-house, but it'd be easy for a hacker to get into. Not only that, because it's in-house, somebody could EMP it and knock out the cameras, and I suspect the alarm system as well."

"I assume they have some sort of fail-safe."

"Big deal. If it goes off, it doesn't matter. The people will grab the artifacts and run before anyone gets there. Also, did you check out the cases?"

"Yeah. Electronic fences."

Shay nodded. "Did you see any evidence in the ground of a rising cage? The ceiling was too high for a dropping cage."

Maria held up a hand. "Hold on a second. Here's what we can do. I can do some quick paperwork to set you up as a consultant. Then I'll grab my badge, and we'll go back for an official inspection, and I can get your comments on the official record."

Shay stared at the cop, incredulity written all her face. "Wait. The police want to pay me money to advise them?"

"This cop does. It won't be a big deal. I've got all sorts of things set up for informants and the like. No one's going to dig deep, if that's what you want."

Maria tried to keep the eagerness out of her voice. She so wanted to go back and shove a report up Spencer Preston's ass, but that didn't change her desire to make sure no one robbed the museum under her watch.

Shay blew out a breath and shrugged. "Why the hell not?"

"How about we meet back here at 4:30? They aren't closing until 6:00 tonight."

"Fine by me." Shay pulled out her phone. "Just need to text Brownstone that I'm gonna help you with something."

5

Outside the tactical room, every sweat-soaked member of the Brownstone Agency was peeling off their jumpsuits. After the first two "magical" battles, they'd fought a few other battles to test new strategies.

James decided choking people out wasn't the best for morale or quick rematches, so he had abandoned that tactic and moved to a focused strategy of ambushing men and killing them with their own weapons. It illustrated the same point about situational awareness without risk of him seriously injuring one of his men by accident.

Trey hung up his jumpsuit and wiped his brow with his sleeve. "Man, I'm fucking tired, and it's not even nighttime yet. I haven't been this tired in a long time." He shook his head at Shorty. "I don't know who has got it worse, us left behind who have to clean up that shit tomorrow because of all the glass, or you poor bastards going to Vegas."

Shorty shrugged. "I like knocking heads in Vegas. A different flavor of scumbag, you know what I'm saying? It gets boring always beating down the local assholes."

Everyone laughed.

Manuel looked at the gathered men. "Why don't we make the team coming back from Vegas do the cleaning?"

"That's kind of a jerk move." Trey shrugged. "'Course it wouldn't hurt to ask them to *help* us clean up."

James finished pulling off his suit. "Oh, that reminds me, Trey. They coming back with my barbeque?"

Trey snorted. "You redefine one-track mind, big man." He laughed. "We're talking about cleaning and bounty hunting, and all you care about is that you get some God Sauce and ribs."

"Now that we're gonna be competing, we need to constantly test the competition. And if you want to be number one, you have to see what the top dogs are already doing." James shrugged. "Plus, this barbeque shit counts as marketing, so we get to write it off. It's smart business."

The other bounty hunter shook his head, a wry smile on his face. "Okay, I'll send them a text to let them know about the barbeque emergency."

James grabbed his phone from the locker and looked down at his messages. He frowned once he spotted the text from Shay.

Ran into Lt. Hall at the museum. Going to help her with a little something. Won't be home until late

"Hall?" James rumbled. "What the fuck is Shay doing with the AET?"

Trey looked at him. "Problem?"

"I don't know. Shay's out with Lieutenant Hall doing…

hell if I know. I get that Hall doesn't want to throw my ass into an ultra-max anymore, but I also know she was just as pissed as Shay about the Lars Hansen shit." James shook his head. "Whatever this shit is, it can't be good for my continued health."

Trey grinned. "Nah, you're overthinking it, big man. The hens got to cluck when the rooster's away, you know what I'm saying? The trick is, the rooster needs to take advantage of that shit, too."

"How?"

"If your woman's busy, we should call up Mack and get together to start planning shit for Saturday."

James nodded. "Good idea."

He stared at his phone, still wondering why his under-the-radar tomb raider and ex-killer girlfriend would be hanging around with an LAPD AET officer on purpose.

Hope this shit doesn't blow up in my face.

Tyler cradled his phone between his cheek and shoulder as he polished the bar. "Really? That many? But nothing about any fives?"

"Yeah," the informant on the other end offered. "That's all the level fours I know are coming to town in the next couple of weeks. I haven't heard shit about any fives, but I don't know if I'd tell you anyway. I'm taking a big risk by telling you all this as it is."

"Risk? What the hell are you talking about? Have I ever fucked you over?" Tyler scoffed. "Even once?"

The informant snorted. "I don't know what to think

about you anymore. The word on the street is that you're Brownstone's bitch now. That you're buddies. Brownstone ain't exactly the friend of the man on the wrong side of the law. And what about Lars Hansen?"

Fuck. Yeah, I'm tired of messing with Brownstone. After that bullshit the government put him through with his kid it's like everyone's against him, and he is a good business partner as long as I show him proper respect.

Tyler snorted. "I make money off Brownstone, sure. Doesn't mean any more than that."

"Just saying," the informant muttered.

"Brownstone's like a hurricane. Unless you're some Oriceran super-elf, you can't fight a hurricane. All I'm trying to do is protect myself from the storm, and maybe make some money selling supplies and information to help protect other people from the storm. If you're a dumbass and you get his attention, that's on you, but I just want to point out, I didn't sell Lars Hansen's location to Brownstone. I called Hansen and offered to tell him where Brownstone was. Hansen knew the score. Even tried to ambush Brownstone. Not my fault he was more talk than walk."

The informant chuckled. "Whatever, man. Just make sure you give me my money. I suppose it don't matter. In the end, you keep paying me, I don't care whose bitch you are."

"Don't worry, you'll be paid the usual way."

"Talk to you later, Mr. Weathervane." The informant hung up.

Tyler tossed the phone into the trash. "Fuck you,

asshole. I hope you dent Brownstone's truck and he punts you through a wall." He frowned. "Just not *my* wall."

Kathy walked over from the other end of the bar and eyed the trash. "A little wasteful." The brunette bartender arched an eyebrow. "Since when do you throw away phones because you're pissed?"

"Not pissed, being careful. It's a burner." Tyler shook his head. "Since I have more money lately, no problem with paying for a little extra security. Only way to make sure we aren't tapped. I'm trying to look into magical options, too. That's what a proper businessman does: expands and protects his investments."

Kathy snickered. "Everything is tapped, or tapped out." She patted a nearby keg. "Like this Guinness is all tapped out. What we really need now is less information-broker-slash-businessman and more strong man to go grab a new keg before the next rush of customers."

She glanced around the room. Even though no one was sitting at the bar, most of the tables were full.

Tyler shrugged. "I'm a lover, not a fighter. Like I'm the strong man to grab a keg."

"Stronger than me." Kathy snorted and shook her head. "With all that talk about Brownstone, maybe you should think about competing with him by hitting the gym. You know, lift a little."

"Damn, that was a low blow. Besides, I'm the boss, and you're my employee, so you should be doing all the heavy lifting."

Kathy scoffed and crossed her arms. "I'm here to serve the customers, listen to their stories, and look hot so they drink more beer. Smelling sweaty ruins my tips." She leaned forward and narrowed her eyes, her voice dropping to a whisper. "And I'm also supposed to be sweetly getting nice little tidbits of info for you. That way you don't have to spend so much on burner phones and informants who piss you off. I'm the one who told you about that triad deal that was going on, and I know you made a nice chunk of change off selling that information. You going to wimp out on me now, Tyler?"

He threw up a hand. "Fine. I'll go get the damned keg. Keep your panties on."

The bartender threw up the hinged gate and stormed toward the hallway leading to the storage room, bathrooms, and his office.

"I need to hire more ditzy chicks as support staff, not ones who are smart enough to come up with counterarguments," he mumbled under his breath. "Instead, my employee's making me do all the hard work."

The bartender moved into the storeroom, located a keg of Guinness, and thanked whoever was in charge of the universe for having the foresight to already have it on a dolly.

"Maybe I could hire a couple of big guys. Nah, that won't work. Then I'll just look weak because I have these big guys around all the time, and they'll cost extra money."

Tyler grabbed the dolly, and with a grunt angled the dolly and keg back. The bartender rolled the dolly out of the storeroom and headed back into the main bar.

A new customer, some guy with too-slick hair and a Hawaiian shirt, sat at the bar.

Kathy leaned over the bar, offering the customer a bright smile. Even though she wore a silk vest and a button-up shirt like Tyler that didn't allow for the display of cleavage, there was more than enough femininity in the brunette's beautiful face to charm a man.

The customer sighed. "Can't you narrow it down for me? You're the bartender. You're supposed to know this stuff."

She fluttered her eyelashes. "You know, even though I'm a bartender, I don't like recommending a particular drink until I really know a customer. Everyone has their own tastes, and until I've seen how they react to different beers, I can't call it."

The customer looked at the bottles and kegs behind her. "You really think it'd help if I ordered three different beers?"

"You're at a bar. The point is to drink booze, right?"

"Okay, give me the three you just mentioned, then."

Kathy stood and grabbed a glass. "Right away, sir."

Tyler pushed the keg over to the bar and flipped up the hinge.

She just got some guy to buy three beers at once by smiling at him and looking pretty. If it weren't for my Brownstone bets, this place would still be a dump. I had a hard time getting guys to buy three beers a night.

Tyler shook his head and moved over to disconnect and pull the old keg out.

I should probably make her the manager. Hire more girls under her, and just sit in the back and do my info broker thing.

He stopped fiddling with the keg for a moment.

Nah, I'm too cheap. That was why I ended up firing all those waitresses and just keeping Kathy.

Tyler looked at the woman. He hoped she never figured out that she could probably start her own place and make a killing.

6

Shay waved to Lieutenant Hall from the steps leading into the museum. The cop still wasn't in uniform, but she did have a badge clipped to her belt and a gun in a holster underneath her jacket.

The AET cop caught up to her and looked around. "Okay, you said security is shitty. Let's take it from the beginning." She pulled out her phone to tap in notes.

The tomb raider smiled. "First of all, look at the sky. What do you see?"

Lieutenant Hall looked up. "Uh, clouds? Buildings in the distance?"

"More to the point, what *don't* you see?"

The cop shrugged. "I don't know. What am I not seeing?"

Shay nodded toward the door and walked that way. "Just saying, if I had rare and valuable artifacts, I'd at least have a few surveillance drones up." She pointed to several camera locations. "Even when they change their angle, they aren't 360 degrees." She cleared her throat. "Plus, they have minimal coverage on the roof."

Lieutenant Hall stared at Shay. "And how the hell do you know that?"

Probably don't want to tell her because I parkoured onto the roof, and I have a world-class hacker on staff.

"You'd be surprised at the kind of things you pick up when you're tomb raiding. One thing is a good appreciation for geometry to lines of sight."

"Tomb raiding?" The cop gave a cool once over. "Or when you're doing other…more illegal things?"

They locked eyes for a moment. The lieutenant was aware of Shay's past life as a killer. She'd said as much to her face, but she'd also told Shay she was willing to let the past stay buried. The tomb raider only hoped that was true.

Lieutenant Hall sighed. "Look, I do need something to put in my notes as an explanation of your expertise."

"Just cite theoretical insufficiencies based on my academic review of tomb raids." Shay winked and opened the door. She gestured the cop through. "Problem number two. Note they only have internal armed protection. There's also no bulletproof booth or anything from which a security guard can return fire. Guns won't mean shit if someone comes in and lays them out with a gun or just blows them up." She gestured toward a guard in the distance. "And they're relying on security by obscurity."

"What do you mean?"

"Those anti-magic deflectors are fakes. They're trying to intimidate mages into being scared, but one quick spell will verify the truth."

Maria snorted. "I *thought* they looked weird."

Shay tapped on the glass of the door. "This isn't bullet-proof, and it's also not truck-proof. If the bad guys knew where to search, they could ram through here and charge straight to the artifacts in under a minute. LAPD will scramble fast, but they aren't going to get here in a couple of minutes."

Maria frowned and nodded.

They moved forward and showed their ticket stubs to the employee at the counter. They continued walking and entered the line for the artifacts.

Shay leaned in to whisper, "This isn't a real choke-point, especially since it's got no line of sight on most of the lobby. That means the bad guys enter armed, rush to the wall, spin around, fire, and they've killed the guards." She gestured at the ceiling. "I don't see any grates that might come down, so once the bad guys waste the arro-gant-ass security in the front, they can stroll in here like nothing."

The lieutenant tapped the notes into her phone. "Fuck, I didn't even think of that."

Shay nodded toward a guard standing where the hallway turned. "He's got his back, not to the wall, but to the hallway. That means, if anyone gets past him—like some hot chick pretending to be a tourist—she can take him out from behind before he knows what's going on. At least the guy in the chair has his back to the wall."

There wasn't much of a line, so they walked straight to the metal detector.

Maria approached the metal detector and pulled out her badge and ID card.

The guard frowned. "Oh, Lieutenant Hall. Mr. Preston

isn't here, but he told us you might stop by. I didn't realize who you were earlier."

"Just doing a quick inspection. You shouldn't have anything to worry about if your security is as good as he claimed."

He waved her through. The detector beeped, but her firearm was obvious.

Shay stepped through. She hadn't brought her gun, fortunately.

Lieutenant Hall nodded toward Shay. "And she's with me."

The guard narrowed his eyes. "You didn't tell Mr. Preston about any undercover officers."

Shay almost laughed at the mistake. She wasn't sure if it were more ridiculous than the idea that an ex-killer-turned-tomb-raider was now helping a cop who'd had it in for her boyfriend until very recently.

Lieutenant Hall shrugged and winked at Shay. "Too bad. Come on, Officer Carson."

The tomb raider smirked as they headed toward the exhibit hall.

Shay pointed to a few windows in the hallway. "Sure, nice natural light, but what good does it do to set up their internal checkpoint when any fool could take out those windows? No bars. Maybe bulletproof, but that doesn't mean they can take an RPG, a rocket, or a fireball."

The cop winced. "Damn."

The other woman turned and shrugged. "You're AET, not a standard cop, which means you're worried about some sort of King Pyro-style asshole showing up—or a Tessa Vansant. Do you think the security you've seen would stop either of those two for more than a few seconds?"

Lieutenant Hall shook her head. "Nope. I don't." She sighed. "Let's continue checking the exhibit hall and then the rest of the museum."

The museum staffer looked between the two women and frowned. "I apologize, Lieutenant Hall, but I need to inform you that we're closing soon."

They'd lost track of time after exploring the rest of the museum, instead falling into idle personal chatter.

She shrugged. "Yeah, I know. Somebody came and told us that a few minutes ago. We're enjoying your lovely lobby for the moment. Thank you."

The staffer frowned, clearly unsure how to best handle the stubborn police officer. He sighed and spun on his heel to storm off.

Shay snickered. "You're gonna piss them off, you know."

"Big fucking deal. They already pissed *me* off." Maria shook her head. "So were you serious? Brownstone is that crappy at understanding women?"

She nodded. "You have to understand, the guy can kick anyone's ass, but the minute a woman or a girl starts crying he doesn't know what to do at all. It's like all of his brain is focused only on how to shoot people and make barbeque."

The cop snorted. "He sounds like a lot of other guys I know. You might think I'm a bitch sometimes, but I have to be to keep the knuckleheads I work with in line. I don't care what people say, it's still hard to be a woman in uniform, especially in something like AET. Half the guys are adrenaline junkies who want to prove how tough they are, and I'm lucky it's only half."

Shay shrugged. "What can you do, Lieutenant? Men need to be men."

"Maria," the cop responded. "Just call me Maria."

"Okay, if you want." The tomb raider eyed her, a hint of suspicion in her gaze. "By the way, what's up with you and Tyler?"

The cop spun, her cheeks reddening. "He's got his good points."

"Just saying, the criminal and the cop?"

"He's barely a criminal." Maria peered at Shay. "And I figure you're probably a more unlikely woman to end up with the country's most famous bounty hunter."

"Touché, Maria. Touché."

Shay had lost track of time again. The lobby lights had been dimmed, and no one else had shown up to complain.

Her phone chimed, and she pulled it out. It was a text from James.

How late?

Late enough. Why?

Okay, just so you know, having a meeting with Mack and Trey. Need to talk BBQ

Shay snorted and texted back.

Fine. I'm gonna go get my own dinner at some vegetarian place just to offset all the meat talk

Your mouth to disappoint

Shay rolled her eyes.

"Problem?" Maria asked.

Shay shook her head. "No. It's just James obsessing over barbeque again. I mean, I've got a thing for thin-crust pizza, but it's nowhere near as crazy as his thing with barbeque. He's got so much barbeque lore stuck in his brain that just kissing him means I could never ever switch to being a vegetarian."

The cop snorted. "I guess there are worse vices."

A guard stepped around the corner with a frown on his face. "You're still here?"

Maria smirked and patted her badge. "What are you going to do, call the cops?"

He looked her up and down as if trying to determine if her badge was fake. "Whatever. If anyone gets upset, I'm throwing you under the bus. I'll let the other guys on duty know what's going on. Don't piss any of them off, and don't, under any circumstances, go into the exhibit room. The wizard put up some sort of spell."

Maria rolled her eyes as the guard turned to saunter toward the hallway.

An odd color reflecting off the top of a metal garbage can nearby caught Shay's attention. She lifted her head. The air above shimmered a faint red.

She'd been on enough tomb raids and run into enough strange magic to recognize a spell when she saw one. The guard yawned as he hit the hallway and then fell to the ground face first.

Knew your fake anti-magic deflectors wouldn't work.

Shay snatched Maria's badge.

"What the hell are you doing?" the cop barked.

"Give me your gun, your wallet, and your phone. Trust me if you don't want to die, and get on the floor fast!"

The cop handed over everything, frowning, then dropped to the floor.

Shay chucked the gun, badge, wallet, and phone across the room. They skittered underneath a vending machine. She then threw her purse behind a nearby garbage can.

She dropped to the ground, hoping no one saw. Otherwise, sleep magic would be the least of her worries.

7

Trey leaned back on James' couch, his hands behind his head. "I don't know about this, big man. The Turf and Surf BBQ championship? The boys ain't ready for that by a long shot. It's like taking a high school team to the Superbowl."

Mack, on the other end of the couch, shook his head. "If we want to represent, we need to go to Del Mar and do just that. The top pitmasters are going to be at that cookoff. Just being there makes a big statement about what PFW is going to bring to the world of barbeque."

Trey frowned. "Won't they just beat our asses?"

"If we go in thinking we're gonna lose, we'll lose," James replied from his recliner. "But I hear what you're saying, and no, I don't think the boys by themselves will be ready. They don't have to be. Mack and I will take the lead this time, and they can just work support. The point is just for them to get experience in a competition setting. Barbeque is a lot like bounty hunting; you've got to keep training in all sorts of environments." He grunted. "Some shit Sun Tzu can't help you with. Barbeque is one of those things."

Trey nodded slowly. "Okay, okay, but how do we even get in? We don't got a top rep for barbeque, so how do we score a slot?"

Mack grinned. "The Brownstone name alone guaranteed us a slot. You think they are going to say no to our boy over there?"

Trey whistled. "Must be nice to be famous."

James grunted. "It's annoying as shit most of the time, but at least it helped here."

The other men chuckled.

Mack turned to Trey. "You ever been to Del Mar?"

Trey shook his head. "Nope."

"It's a nice place, and the cookoff is right on the water, so it'll be a cool place to cook. The guys will love it."

"Okay, Mack, James, you've sold me." Trey shrugged. "And I'll sell it to the boys." He glanced down at his watch. "I've got some shit to take care of still tonight, and I've got a tactical room to help clean up tomorrow. We about done here?"

James nodded. "Yeah."

The junior bounty hunter rose and gave a mock salute. "See you around. Sergeant. Big man." He headed to the front door, stepped outside, and closed it softly behind him.

Mack stared at the door for a moment. "I would never have believed it last year, you know. It's almost a miracle."

"Believed what?"

"Trey Garfield and his boys all being right and proper with the law." The cop blew out a breath. "Not saying they were ever true garbage like the Demon Generals or some of the other local gangs, but they were moving that way. Maybe a year more, and they would have been serious trash. I think if they had been in any other neighborhood, they might have started doing stuff they couldn't come back from. You were here, so they couldn't act up too much."

"No one can change the past. Just have to keep moving forward. They're all good bounty hunters now. Hell, if anything, they're more restrained than I am. They haven't killed anyone yet, and some of those assholes really have it coming."

"For a man who always claims he doesn't care about anything unless there's a bounty involved, you've sure done a lot to help the community."

"I'm still a bounty hunter. I just realized that a few more people having my back isn't a bad thing." James shrugged. "And helping lead Trey and his boys to kick bounty ass was easy. It's not like I'm sending them all to become rock stars or some shit."

Mack laughed. "True enough. Just saying, Brownstone, no problem having a little pride in what you've done. You're slowly cleaning up L.A. I heard some AET types talking the other day about how a lot of high-level bounties won't even show up now because they're afraid of you."

"Good. They should be afraid." He glowered at the floor.

"If we end up with a city where an army of Brownstone-affiliated bounty hunters controls half the crime and your reputation keeps the big freaks out of town, the cops can do the rest. We can become the safest damned city in the United States.'

James grunted and shrugged. "I just do what I do. I don't have any big plans."

"Don't want to run for mayor someday or something? It's like Trey said. You're famous." Mack shrugged.

The bounty hunter grimaced. "Politics? I'd sooner hunt nothing but level-six monsters in the sewer for the rest of my life. At least they're honest about being scum."

"Good answer." Mack grinned. "Oh, I also have to thank you for something else."

"What?"

"Heather."

The bounty hunter furrowed his brow. "What about her?"

"She's a model renter. No complaints, paid several months in advance, and, you know, I like the idea that I'm helping a single mom. Not that I didn't like helping you, but your daughter wasn't living with you at the time. I've had trouble in the past with that unit. It helps that I'm a cop, so people don't want to get too rowdy, but with you and now her it's been damned easy."

James nodded. "Glad to hear that. She's had a tough time, and moving here is helping her start her life over."

"Fine by me. Almost makes me want to look into getting some more apartments to rent out. It'd be nice to have some additional income when I retire. I just need twelve more like Heather, and I could buy an entire apartment complex."

The bounty hunter shook his head. "Sounds annoying and complicated."

"Most things worth doing are, Brownstone."

Shay blinked her eyes open. No headache, no pain. The spell must have just been simple sleep magic. Her hands were bound in handcuffs, and her legs tied.

I never thought the assholes would hit the museum that quickly. The exhibit just opened. I wish I'd brought my magical lockpick.

She looked around. Maria lay next to her, unconscious. From the looks of things they were in the back of a large van, but no one else was there or anything but a few reflectors.

Not much to work with. Damn, hate it when the other guys are thorough.

Shay peered closer at Maria's cuffs. A light glow surrounded them.

Fuck. Magically locked. I'll give these guys credit. They're really good. Don't even know if my lockpick would have worked against them.

A man's voice drifted from the front. "Why did we have to get stuck carrying these bitches? They were out already when we grabbed them. Should have left them there."

"The boss says they're out of place. Plus, they might be witnesses."

"Out of place?" The first man snorted. "What the fuck does that mean?"

"Four guards in there, all in uniform, and two random women? They don't look like museum people. Something about them made the boss worry. Just be glad we only had to carry two, and not them plus the guards. Those guys were real heavy, at least according to Joey's bitching."

Shay grimaced. The worst thing you could run into were intelligent criminals. Getting rid of the lieutenant's badge and their IDs had at least delayed identification, which would give them time. Maybe they wouldn't care about someone who was officially a professor, but a cop probably wouldn't last long.

"Whatever," the second criminal muttered. "I want to finish this job and get the hell out of this city. I've got money to spend."

The two men fell quiet. The van pulled to a stop, and Shay heard a metal warehouse door opening. Shay knew the sound all too well from her own warehouses.

Okay, so we're already at a drop point or a base, but the guy said he wanted to get the hell out of the city. So we're still in LA. Probably means Maria and I were out for less than two hours. If we're still in LA, I still have a chance of calling James in if I can't figure out a way out of this myself.

The van pulled forward and then stopped again. It shook for a moment as the two men exited, and the slamming of their doors confirmed it seconds later.

Maria opened her eyes and scowled. She took in the back of the van and scowled harder.

"Two men up front," Shay whispered. "From what I heard, they mainly took us because they thought we looked out of place, but they've got all the night guards, too. That means whoever is organizing this is worried about loose ends."

"Why the hell did you throw all my stuff away?" Maria

lifted her head to glare at her. "We might have had a chance."

"They came in with magic. Come on, you're AET. You know better. Do you take on enhanced threats with your 9mm? It's a peashooter against serious magic, not a railgun. Besides, I saw the guard go down and figured a sleep spell was coming. Even if you had a railgun, it wouldn't do you any good asleep."

Maria sighed and let her head fall back on the rubber mat on the floor of the van. "The badge? My wallet? Your purse? What was getting rid of all that about?"

Shay shrugged, which made the cuffs tug on her wrists. "Didn't want them to ID us. As long as they don't know what's up with either of us, we have a better chance of staying alive. "We don't want them to know who you are, in particular. My identity's hidden a little better."

"Then who I am supposed to be? A junior tomb raider?"

Shay snickered. "Sorry. Already have an apprentice."

Maria rolled her eyes.

Shay took a deep breath. "Don't worry. I've got a plan, but I'll need you to trust me."

"I already disarmed myself at your request. That's some pretty fucking major trust. If you get me killed, I'm going to haunt your ass until *you* get killed, and then Brownstone after that."

"Don't worry, I'm not getting killed in some skeevy warehouse by these assholes. I've got too much pride for that."

Someone slammed a door nearby. They didn't have much time.

Shay locked eyes with Maria. "Here's my plan…"

Mack gave James a wave and closed the door behind him.

The bounty hunter yawned and looked down at his phone. It was almost ten. It'd been a good night of barbeque planning and talking with two men he now considered friends.

He frowned.

Shay said she would be out with Hall, but I didn't figure she'd be this late, and she knew we were staying at my place tonight.

James picked up his phone to check for calls or texts he might have missed. Nothing. The last text he'd received from Shay hours ago concerned her threat of going to the most unholy of restaurants, a vegetarian place.

Some things just shouldn't exist.

"A little text wouldn't hurt. If anything, it might stop them from whatever they're planning to do to me. According to the podcast, more communication will show I care."

Hey, Shay. When are you coming home?

The bounty hunter made a quick trip to the kitchen to grab a bottle of Irish Dry Stout before returning to his living room. He took a few sips of his beer and lifted his phone.

Still no response.

Maybe she's out dancing. Some sort of girls' night.

James grunted. If Shay wanted to party, that was fine, and if Maria Hall or any of Shay's other friends could save him from having to go dancing, that made him really happy. His most recent experience with forced clubbing by Shay had only reminded him how annoying it was to be in a crowded place with loud music.

At least at the Leanan Sídhe, they didn't pound into your skull with their stereo.

What the fuck do I do? Should I go to bed, or will she be pissed if I go to bed without her? I don't want to fuck this up. Wait, maybe Alison could give me some advice.

James grunted. It was too late to call Alison, given the time zone difference. Not only that, she'd texted him earlier to say she would be very busy the next few days with the school year starting up.

Muttering, the bounty hunter picked up his remote control and turned on the TV. Maybe a halfway-decent cooking show was on and could distract him for a few minutes.

A harried-looking male reporter appeared on the screen in front of the Los Angeles Museum of Natural History. The TV was muted.

"Huh. They doing a story on those artifacts?"

James frowned. That didn't seem right. It was night, and a dozen cop cars with flashing lights surrounded the museum. His gaze dipped to the chyron.

Breaking news: Daring theft of Oriceran artifacts from the Los Angeles Natural History Museum.

The bounty hunter turned on the sound.

The reporter held his microphone close to his face. "Details are still being released about a brazen robbery some are already calling the crime of the century. The four night guards aren't accounted for, and blood was found on the scene. We've received conflicting reports about other potential kidnap victims, but the police are being very tight-lipped about that at this time, along with exactly what's been taken. They've verified that the Oriceran artifact exhibit was indeed the target of this crime, and they have confirmed that magic was used in the commission of the robbery."

James muted the TV and grunted. He believed in God, not coincidence. Shay had mentioned checking out the museum, and a bunch of magical artifacts sounded just like the kind of thing Lieutenant Hall would worry about and go poke her nose into.

He picked up his phone, wondering if he could call the police, but shook his head. If anything had happened to Shay, he would spill so much blood the Pacific Ocean would turn red, and he couldn't have any cops getting in his way.

Even if she hadn't been hurt, the cops had too many restrictions and procedures to follow. They were good men and women, but they could be too slow because of those rules.

He marched over to his door and pulled his keys off a pegboard.

James patted the amulet underneath this shirt.

You're gonna get to come out real soon, I think.

8

T yler whistled and shook his head as he watched the news report on the robbery. "Wonder if any of those level fours had anything to do with that?"

He frowned. It always annoyed him when something big happened and he couldn't find a way to make money off it. He'd gotten too dependent on Brownstone. He needed to diversify his revenue streams.

A hush fell over the bar, and the hairs on the back of his neck stood up.

Shit. What now?

The bartender slowly turned around to find James Brownstone standing in front of him.

Of course. Can't think of the Devil without him appearing.

"We need to talk," the bounty hunter rumbled.

Yeah, this is going to do wonders for my rep of being his bitch. You know what? Fuck them. Besides, just because I need more revenue streams doesn't mean I should ignore the one that walked right up to me.

Tyler offered him a grin. "Most times we talk lately, I make money." He gave a quick nod to Kathy and headed toward the hallway. "Come on, Brownstone. Let's talk in private."

The bounty hunter strode behind him, his eyes narrowed and his nostrils flared. Tyler swallowed.

Fuck. Did I do something to piss him off? He looks like he wants to kill someone. I haven't done shit to him. I've bent over backward to be nice.

Tyler led Brownstone into his office, and both men took a seat.

"What's up, Brownstone?"

James grunted. "Do you know where Lieutenant Hall is?"

Tyler shrugged. "Not really."

"But you have a way of getting in contact with her?" The bounty hunter's heavy gaze unsettled the information broker.

Tyler dialed her normal number. After several rings, it went to voicemail.

He hesitated, then pulled another phone out of his desk.

She said this was supposed to be in case of emergencies, but Brownstone looking like he's going to murder me is most definitely a damned emergency.

He dialed and waited. It rang and rang. No response.

What, no voicemail on the emergency phone? Useless.

"Shit," Tyler muttered, licking his lips. He needed to give Brownstone something if he wanted to survive the next few minutes. "She's not answering. I don't know what to tell you, Brownstone. All I can do is call her. It's not like we live together."

Brownstone grunted, the murderous gleam in his eye

intensifying. "Fine, if you don't know where she is, do you know where she was supposed to be?"

Tyler snorted. "I deal in information, not stalking. What the fuck is this about, Brownstone? I thought we had some sort of truce semi-partnership thing going on, and now you're storming in here acting like you're going to kick my ass."

The bounty hunter jerked his thumb in the general direction of the main bar. "You were watching the news about the robbery when I came in."

"Yeah, what of it? I didn't know shit about it if that's what you're asking. That's kind of a sore point, if you really want to know."

Brownstone hands curled into fists. "I can't get hold of Shay. She told me earlier she was gonna check out that museum, and later she texted me to say she needed to help Hall with something. Now the news is mentioning someone might have been kidnapped. You put the fucking puzzle together."

Tyler ran a hand through his hair. "Shit, shit, and more shit. You're serious?"

"Do I fucking *look* like I'm joking?"

The information broker stared at Brownstone and took in the anger in the other man's face. The bounty hunter had killed hundreds of men over the murder of his dog. If someone killed his girlfriend, LA might be in its final days of existence. Still, there were other considerations, and it was up to Tyler to point them out.

He took a deep breath and slowly let it out. "Look, Brownstone, we can't assume that they were grabbed from the museum. For all we know, they're at a Chippendales show enjoying beefcake on the side."

Brownstone's only response was a deep grunt.

Shit. I think I'm making it worse. Does the end of LA start with the end of my bar?

Tyler held up a hand. "I don't know much about your woman, but she's *your* woman, which means she probably kicks ass. And just from what I've seen, she's tough."

Brownstone nodded. "She knows how to take care of herself. Not denying that."

"Exactly, and I've seen Maria take on guys bigger than her in this very bar. Even without her armor and guns, she's tough. Tougher than me, honestly." Tyler shrugged. "So I'm not even sure we should try to save them. And that's assuming they even were kidnapped."

"What the fuck are you saying?" Brownstone growled.

Tyler held up a hand. "Hear me out. They might already be handling this and kicking the shit out of everyone who dared lay a finger on them. If we go riding in there on our white horses, they'll just laugh their asses off at us. We'll piss them off and accomplish nothing."

Brownstone shrugged. "They will always be laughing at us for being dumbasses. What's new about that? I'm never gonna apologize for protecting my woman. What about you? You a man, or a cowardly piece of shit who'll leave his woman in the cold rather than risk his ass?"

Tyler stared at the bounty hunter, his mouth open. He wanted to be pissed, but the rebuke stung. He gritted his teeth.

I should just leave it to him. This isn't my problem. Maria's just a friend and a cop. Maybe a business acquaintance. Not some intelligent, sexy, kick-ass woman I dream about.

"Fuck!" Tyler shouted. He scrubbed a hand over his face. "Okay, I fucking admit it. I've got it bad for Maria, okay? You happy?" He slammed a hand on the desk. "Fucking feelings. Useless. No money in them."

A hint of a smile appeared on Brownstone's face. "Keep this shit up, and I might actually respect you. So, you gonna help save them?"

Tyler stood. "Let me go take care of something, and I'll come back to discuss this in a few minutes."

Brownstone nodded.

A minute later, James pulled out his phone. Tyler had sources, and so did he. The bounty hunter pulled up his contacts list and prepared to call Heather.

He sighed.

Nah. She's just getting some time with her son. If I pull her into this, it's not fair to him.

James dialed Peyton instead.

"Good evening, Herr Brownstone," the hacker responded in an awful German accent. "To what do I owe the pleasure on this fine LA night?"

That guy's a good hacker, but damn *is he obnoxious at times.*

"Do you know where Shay is?"

"I thought she was looking into that museum with that cop, Hall." The fake German accent had disappeared.

James grunted. "Look up the fucking news for LA."

Peyton sighed. "It's late at night, and I was in the middle

of something. One second." He hissed. "Shit, this isn't good."

"I tried calling her, but I can't get her. I need you to figure out if she got taken out of the museum and where she is. Just get the location, and I'll do the rest."

Peyton took a deep breath. "Full scourge mode?"

"If I need to. Maybe just showing up will convince the fuckers to surrender."

"Okay, I'm on it. I'll call you as soon as I know what's up." The hacker ended the call.

James' hand drifted to the amulet underneath his shirt.

You're always wanting me to kill people. Guess you're gonna get your wish soon.

The bounty hunter took several deep breaths, clenching and unclenching his fists. He needed a target for all his frustration and building emotions.

Several minutes later, Tyler opened the office door and strolled back in. "Okay. I've closed the Black Sun. Everyone got a free drink, along with a credit for a few others, and were asked to leave. Kathy's going to close up for me, and she's trying to do damage control on rumors."

"Rumors?"

The information broker smirked. "Yeah. Apparently, they all think we're concocting another pay-per-view event or a way to get your girlfriend more pissed off at you. A couple of others had more colorful theories."

"Like what?"

"That I've fallen in love with your uber-manliness. That I'm gay for Brownstone."

James chuckled. "When I first met Shay, she thought I was gay because I didn't hit on her."

Tyler raised an eyebrow. "You know, when I first met her, not saying I didn't give her a little look or two. She's damned hot, but I wasn't ready to touch her brand of angry. I'm not the kind of guy who purposely causes myself harm." He laughed. "Ironic, since you're with her now."

James' phone rang with a call from Peyton. He held up a hand and used the other one to grab his phone.

"What do you got?" the bounty hunter asked.

"According to the video, Shay and Lieutenant Hall entered the museum, but they never left."

James grunted. "Never left? What the fuck does that mean? The cops are all over the museum, and they didn't find anyone there."

"Well, that's what someone wanted us to think, anyway. I was able to figure out that there was a six-minute splice in the video feed, so anyone could have entered or left during that time and we wouldn't know. I've traced Shay's phone to the police station. Same thing with Lieutenant Hall's."

James' grip on the phone tightened. "And you're sure the cops don't have her? Maybe they're holding her as a suspect or some shit. I can go talk to them. They might listen to me."

"Nope. The LAPD is spun up like a bunch of very angry hornets. They apparently found Hall's badge and gun on scene. They're keeping it quiet for now, but I think they're worried they're going to find a dead cop soon. Once that happens, things are going to get really heavy."

James blew out a breath. "And you're not feeding me a line? You're not responsible for that six-minute slice? Trying to protect Shay, maybe?"

Peyton snorted. "Look, when you called, I was just finishing pizza with my girlfriend and looking forward to a bit of strip Twister. Now you tell me someone might have snatched Shay during some museum heist. This isn't any more fun for me than it is for you."

Strip Twister? How the fuck does that even work?

James shook his head. "Just keep digging and see if you can find me any clues. There has to be something there we could use. They couldn't have shut down all the video feeds for that long without someone noticing."

"Will do. Don't worry, Brownstone. I've got this."

The bounty hunter ended the call and shook his head.

Tyler's eyes narrowed. "From what I overheard, it sounds like you've got exactly jack and shit to go off of."

James shrugged. "We know it took them under six minutes to pull off their heist and get away."

The other man nodded. "You're a bounty hunter. I'm the information broker. I'll see what I can do."

Logan paced back and forth, waiting for the video call to connect.

Why does he also want to do a video call? I hate video calls. Is this just about him seeing me squirm? Fucker. Someday I'll be the one calling the shots.

The call connected, and a scarred dwarf frowned at the man on the screen. "The news is interesting this evening, Logan. My question to you is if you recovered the items in question."

"Yeah, we got the circlet and everything else, just like

you told us to, Tak. Complete damned success." Logan grinned. "It was almost too easy, thanks to all our...special preparations."

The dwarf's lips curled into a sneer. "Good. You'll be rewarded for your success. I also heard on the news that four guards are missing. What other complications were there? There are always some."

He probably already knows. Is this another test? Fucker.

Logan shrugged. "Six witnesses. At least maybe they are. We don't know how long it took before the spell knocked their asses out. Three of the guards went down quick, and one guard was a wizard. He managed a counter-spell, but we shot him before he could do much. He's still alive, and he wasn't able to call the cops. We were long gone by the time the alarms went off."

The dwarf furrowed his brow. "Six witnesses, but you only mentioned four guards. Who else then was present?"

"Two chicks we found up front. Don't know who they are. Weren't dressed like staff or guards. Didn't have any ID on them. That made me more than a little suspicious." Logan shrugged. "Half-wonder if they are private security specialists or someone like that."

Tak nodded. "And what do you think we should do with them, Logan?"

The human shrugged. "We don't know what they saw. Even with the masks, somebody might be able to pull some magic shit. I think we should kill 'em and leave them in the warehouse for someone to find a few months from now when we're all the fuck away from LA."

Tak scratched his bearded chin. "A possibility, but I don't like loose ends."

"All the more reason to kill them. Leave no loose ends, guards or women."

The dwarf shook his head. "Not until we know who everyone is, especially these women. They might even be worth money. They could be nothing more than idiot tourists who got lost, or they might be someone far more valuable. Keep them alive until you have a better idea who they are."

"And the guards?"

"Find out more about them, but I'll leave that matter to your discretion." The dwarf gave him a sinister grin. "Don't disappoint me."

9

Shay took a deep breath. Timing would be everything for the plan. She could control herself, but she wondered if the cop, who was used to taking charge, would be able to wait until the right time. They needed maximum surprise when an appropriate opportunity presented itself.

She could make out voices from just beyond the doors. A second later, the doors opened, and two men in ski masks appeared, one with a large knife.

He pointed the knife at Shay, then Maria. "Boss says to keep you alive for right now, but if you pull any bullshit, you're dead. Got me?"

The two women gave shallow nods.

The man leaned over and sliced the ropes at their feet.

Maria looked at Shay, and the tomb raider shook her head.

Not the time, Maria. Not yet. Bide our time until we have a good chance.

"Move," the man barked.

The women scooted out of the back of the van. They

were in a large warehouse, as Shay had suspected, with four other identical vans being packed with boxes.

The men pulled out guns and nodded toward a hallway across the loading bay. Shay and Maria started moving.

Several masked men were opening other boxes and applying decals to the vans to make them appear to be Andercarr delivery vans.

Guess UPS should be happy the bad guys aren't pretending to be them.

She resisted a snicker. She needed to focus and pump these assholes for information.

"What's gonna happen to us?" Shay asked.

"You don't need to know that. Just behave, and maybe you'll make it out of this in one piece. Sorry, chick, wrong place, wrong time."

I'm gonna be the one saying that sooner than later, asshole, when I shove a knife into your throat.

Shay and Maria exchanged glances. There were a dozen men in the room, not counting the two escorting them. Even if they could somehow get free of the handcuffs, the women didn't have any weapons. Any attempt to break free at that moment would be suicidal.

They made it to the hallway. Halfway down it, they turned into a smaller hallway and finally arrived at a storage-room door.

One of the men pulled out a palm-sized golden disk inscribed with the Seal of Solomon. He held it against the door, and it glowed for a second before the lock clicked.

He opened the door and shoved them both inside. Before they could even turn around, he'd closed the door. The door glowed, and the lock clicked again.

Definitely not your standard-issue thieves if they have artifacts like that.

Three security guards knelt around the room. One lay on the ground. Shay recognized him as the wizard from the exhibit hall. Blood soaked his shirt and jacket, probably from the bullet wound in his shoulder. He was pale and unconscious but breathing.

Maria turned to Shay. "Even if that's their whole team outside, these aren't some fly-by-night dustheads looking to score. We're going to have to be careful about all this."

The tomb raider nodded. "Very professional job. If they've got one artifact, they've probably got more, not to mention whatever they got from the museum."

"We need to get this shit done," yelled a gruff voice on the other side of the door. "We're on the clock, you fucking idiots."

Maria frowned. "The only thing I don't get is, why bring us along?"

Shay rolled her shoulders. The handcuffs were getting annoying, and her shoulders were cramping. For all she knew, one of them was in on it.

"That's the thing about magic. It can be unpredictable. They're probably not sure what everybody saw."

"Why not just kill us?"

"Don't know. It might be they don't know who we are."

Maria nodded to the guards. "*They* know who we are."

The guard from the lobby looked up, his eyes wide. "You're a cop, right? You have some sort of implant they can track or something?"

Shay stomped over to him and glared down at him. "Shut your fucking mouth. If they find out who she is, she's dead, and if she's dead, you're going down with her. Understand, asshole?"

He winced and nodded.

Maria sighed and shook her head. "We're on our own here." She gazed at Shay. "Looks like stage one of your plan is working well enough. Now we at least have an idea what and who we're dealing with."

"Yep. Guns. Low-level magic. All humanoid."

The guard yelped. "What do you mean. 'all humanoid?'"

Shay shrugged at him. "If there's magic involved, it can mean anything from a wizard to some weird-ass Oriceran monster who is nothing but nightmare fuel."

He looked down. "I don't want to die."

"Then shut up and be quiet while the grown-ups figure out how to escape." Shay looked at Maria. "As I told you in the van, we just need to wait for our chance. If we can get free of these cuffs and take out one of the guards, at least we'll have a weapon. Once I have a weapon or two, well, I can use some of the old skills."

Maria snickered. "I never thought I'd look forward to that so much."

James frowned down at his phone. He'd called the Professor twice, and it went to voice mail both times. At this time of night, Smite-Williams was almost always at the pub. Even when he was drunk enough to bring out Father O'Banion, he usually answered his phone.

Damn it. I don't have time to fuck around, old man. I don't care how drunk you are. Answer your fucking phone already.

The bounty hunter glanced toward the main bar. Tyler was on his phone, his brow furrowed while he gesticulated wildly.

We're both working contacts. There's no fucking way we won't be able to track them down. I'm the damned Scourge of Harriken. The fucking Granite Ghost. I can find Shay and Hall.

James sighed and shook his head. Time for call attempt number three. He lifted the phone, and a call came in from the Professor.

"Finally," he rumbled. He hit the button to accept the call. "Professor."

"Ah, sorry, lad. I was transfixed by this rather unfortunate spectacle of the museum robbery." There was a gulp from the other end. Beer, no doubt. "Maybe you were calling on Miz Carson's behalf? I'm more than willing to pay top dollar if either of you would take on a quick job to track down the stolen merchandise. From what little I've gleaned, this is not a good group of artifacts to let bad men get away with. The Circlet of the Lost Gnome King could, in the wrong hands, wipe a lot of people's memories—like those of everyone in California. And that's just one of the artifacts."

James grunted. "Shay was..." He shook his head. "If you can get me something that'll let me track the artifact down quickly, I'll be happy to take the job and take out whoever gets in my way."

"Ah, good, lad. I can have something like that in my possession shortly to pass along to you. How quickly can either you or Miz Carson get there?" Another gulp followed.

Always got to keep the right priorities, huh, Professor?

James chuckled. "Shay will be in the thick of it, I promise, but I'll be there as soon as possible to pick up the artifact. After that, I'm off to save Californians' memories."

"See you soon, James."

The bounty hunter ended the call and frowned, wondering if he needed heavier weapons than the .45 and the few knives he had in his truck.

Fuck. I don't have time to stop off at the warehouse. I've got Whispy Doom, and that's all I really need. If I can take out a Drow queen, I can take on some museum thieves.

James stepped into the main bar.

"Any information on the thieves will be rewarded," Tyler said into his phone. "And I'm willing to pay a premium. Yes. Yes, I understand that. Just get me the fucking information."

James nodded to Tyler and motioned to the front door. The bartender nodded back. He grabbed something from under the bar and stuck it in his waistband.

The bounty hunter couldn't make it out, but he didn't worry about Tyler's weapon choice.

It didn't matter. He needed the man's information. James would take care of all the necessary ass-kicking and killing.

The former enemies now frenemies made their way out of the Black Sun and to the bounty hunter's F-350.

"The famous ancient truck," Tyler mumbled. "Never thought I'd ride in it." He chuckled. "At least not without handcuffs."

James unlocked the passenger door and then circled around to the driver's side.

Tyler settled into his seat and put on his seatbelt.

Caution when driving with James Brownstone was always warranted.

"Where we going?" the information broker asked.

James started the truck. "The Leanan Sídhe."

Tyler winced. "I'll stay in the truck when we get there."

The bounty hunter eyed him for a moment. He didn't know about any bad blood between either the pub and Tyler or the Professor and Tyler, but considering all the deals that went down at the Leanan Sídhe, he wasn't that surprised that the owner of the Black Sun might have run into trouble with the other place.

Right now, James needed all the help he could get, and not only that, Tyler had a right to help rescue Maria. He wouldn't press him on what the problem was.

"I've got a line on an artifact that should help us track the women," James explained. "And I can get that from someone at the Leanan Sídhe."

"Smite-Williams," Tyler muttered.

"Yeah." James arched a brow and pulled out of the parking lot. Tyler was more well-informed than the bounty hunter had realized.

They arrived at the pub.

James threw open the door and nodded to Tyler. "This won't take long."

The information broker nodded back. "I'm not going anywhere."

The bounty hunter slammed his door shut and hurried into the pub. The typical thick crowd choked the place, and he all but charged toward the back where the Professor sat with a small box on the table in front of him.

The bounty hunter didn't even bother to sit. He pointed to the box. "That it?"

The Professor opened the box. A silver crucifix lay inside.

James narrowed his eyes. "What's this?"

"It belonged to Saint Anthony, lad."

The bounty hunter chuckled. "That's appropriate. How do you use it? Just pray to him?"

"That might help, but it also gets warmer the closer you get to the object of your search." The Professor shrugged. "Be aware that it gets really hot. Burn-your-hands hot."

James grabbed the crucifix. "I'm not worried. I'm the driver, and I'm Catholic."

"Also note, this thing only works on objects, not people. I suggest focusing on the circlet. That's the most powerful of the stolen artifacts. You'll get the best resonance that way."

With a quick nod to the Professor, he spun on his heel and marched for the door, ignoring all the noise and din of the pub to offer a silent prayer to the patron saint of all things lost.

The bounty hunter hopped back into his truck and handed Tyler the crucifix.

The information broker took it. "It's slightly warm. What's this?"

"It'll get warmer as we get closer to the main artifact. From there, we can find the people who might have taken Shay and Hall and break their bones until they give up their location." James frowned. "By the way, I've done this kind of tracking before in Vegas. It's annoying as f—"

He eyed the crucifix. He didn't know if its power came from secular magic or a true divine blessing, but there was no problem with being cautious and hoping for a little help from the Man Upstairs or his saints.

"It's annoying," James finished. "If we can just get a general direction, it will help a lot."

Tyler nodded. "I'm waiting for some calls."

As if his words had summoned it, James' phone rang with a call from Peyton. He grabbed it and put it to his ear.

"Tell me you have something useful," the bounty hunter rumbled.

"I was checking feeds from drones in the area. There was a mysterious failure of several drones around the same time as the missing video footage. Not sure if it was EMP or magic. Anyway, I found a drone farther out, grabbed the footage, and enhanced it. Spotted a few suspicious vans all going northbound on the 110." Peyton sighed. "But that's all I've got. I haven't been able to find any more sign of them."

James grunted. "A general direction is all we need. Thanks." He hung up. "We go north from the museum and head toward the 110. Pay the fu— Pay attention to that thing and tell me if it gets warmer."

The bounty hunter pulled his truck away from the curb and started heading north while also gradually making his way closer to the 110.

Minutes later, Tyler cleared his throat. "It's getting warmer, I think."

James nodded. "Good."

He gunned the truck through the streets, the powerful engine roaring in the night. If there were ever a time he needed the cops to look the other way, this was it.

Just need to get to her before it's too late. That's all I ask.

"North from the museum isn't all that specific, Brownstone." Tyler frowned. "Do we have any other information on where the women or the artifacts might be?"

"That's why we have the crucifix." James shrugged. "Just keep paying attention to it."

Miles later, Tyler's phone chimed. He pulled it out with his free hand and put to his ear.

"Yes. I understand. Thanks. You'll be paid using the standard method within twelve hours with a bonus." The information broker slipped the phone back into his pocket. "Okay, I owe someone a lot of money, but they've given me a useful tip that should narrow down the search."

James glanced at him. "What?"

"The vans we're looking for were spotted in Koreatown. If we didn't have your holy doodad that'd be too big an area to search, but with this little thing, I think we have a chance." Tyler held up the crucifix.

The bounty hunter grunted. "That belonged to Saint Anthony. Show some respect."

Tyler frowned at the cross. "This is an actual holy artifact?"

"Yeah."

The information broker grimaced. "If I hold it for too long, it's not going to, you know, turn me all religious, is it?" He eyed James. "Is that what happened to you?"

James snorted. "I was raised by priests, idiot."

"Must have been the vengeful kind."

By the time they took an exit off the 110 into Koreatown, the increasing heat of the crucifix forced Tyler to hold it using a handkerchief.

"This thing is really starting to burn, Brownstone. I don't know how much longer I can handle this."

"Don't be such a pussy." James nodded. "And, yeah, the Professor mentioned it might do that. Specifically called it 'burn-your-hands hot.'"

Tyler rolled his eyes. "And you didn't think to tell me? Why can't *you* hold it?"

"Because I'm driving."

"We can take turns driving, asshole."

James barked out a laugh. "I truly love three things in this world: Shay, my daughter, and this truck. No way you're driving my truck while I'm still breathing. I believe in monogamy."

Tyler sighed and looked down at the crucifix. "How hot can it get? It's not going to blow up, is it?"

"Maybe."

"*Maybe*? What the hell, Brownstone?"

James shrugged. "I've seen tracking artifacts work that

way before. The closer you get, the more they react. Then boom."

Tyler laughed. "You're just screwing me, aren't you, Brownstone?"

"Nope. Had it happen once."

The information broker groaned. "Fuck my life."

S hay sighed.

This is what I get for not hiding a knife in my boot. Good thing I didn't have one of my adamantine knives in my purse. I might never see it again. It's like the universe is punishing me for daring to not be armed.

She glanced at Maria. The cop watched the door, a scowl fixed on her face. Being a hostage probably wasn't a familiar thing for the strong-willed AET lieutenant.

It wasn't exactly like Shay'd had experience with being a hostage, but given that her day job involved everything from ghosts to demonic chickens, it was hard to get too worked up about anything less weird. This whole experience didn't even make her top ten of potentially lethal ends.

Shay and Maria sat against the wall. They'd stopped talking. There wasn't much point until the situation changed.

The door glowed, and the lock clicked. Two masked men entered. Both held guns.

"We need some information," one of the men announced. "You resist, you die right here. Understand?"

I'm so gonna enjoy gutting you, asshole. You think you're tough? You have no fucking idea what tough is. And that's me. James will grind you into paste if he finds you.

Everyone nodded, including Shay.

The thug smiled. "Good. That makes this shit easy. None of you fuckers had your wallets on you." The masked man glared at one of the guards. "Why not?"

The guard swallowed. "We're not supposed to have anything in our pockets during our shift other than our access key cards. Mr. Preston was very insistent on that."

Maria snorted. "Fucking pompous asshole," she whispered under her breath. "This is *his* fault. Should have had more protection."

The masked man spun toward Shay. "And what about you bitches? Why didn't you have your purses and shit?"

The tomb raider kept her face neutral and shrugged. "Must have dropped them when we passed out from whatever it is that you guys did."

The man nodded. "Okay, the next part is pretty damned simple. You're all gonna give me your names. If you refuse, you die." He pointed his gun at Shay. "Your name first. I don't like the defiance I see in your eyes."

"Zoe Davis." The tomb raider offered the lie with ease.

You assholes think you can spook me? I've been faking my identity for half my life. I have a whole annex filled with fake identities.

"And why the fuck were you at the museum, Zoe?"

"Because it had cool magical artifacts." Shay shrugged. "That was kind of the point of the exhibit."

His face twitched, and she wondered if she'd stepped over the line.

Fuck it. If I'm gonna die, I'm gonna die. I'm not cowering in front of some asshole lackey just because he has a gun.

The man snorted and turned toward Hall. "And you?"

"Consuela Ramirez," the cop offered, not a hint of doubt on her face. "I'm a friend of Zoe's. I'm not much for museums, but she convinced me to go. Let me just say, I'm really, really regretting that choice."

She's better at this than I thought. Good at lying and kicking ass. She might have made a good professional killer in another life.

The masked thug asked each of the guards the same question. The last of the three conscious guards offered the name of the unconscious wizard.

The interrogator turned to his friend. "Go ask if he gives a shit about any of these people."

The other thug nodded and hurried out of the room.

Shay shifted slightly. This might be their chance to escape, but she wasn't sure. It didn't smell right. They could take out the single guard and get a weapon, but the other guard would be coming back soon, meaning a greater chance of the others being alerted.

The door flew open less than a minute after the other man had left.

The second masked thug frowned. "Leave them for now. One of the artifacts is acting strangely. The boss wants everyone out there in case something happens."

The first thug snorted and shot a sneer at the hostages. "This shit isn't over. We'll be back soon, and some of you might be dead not long after that."

One of the guards whimpered as both the thugs departed.

Shay and Maria exchanged glances. The situation finally smelled right.

The tomb raider leaned forward. "They're distracted. I think we'll have our chance soon. Get ready."

Logan opened the nondescript box in the back of the van and frowned down at the circlet lying in the box in a sea of packing peanuts. The scent of burnt cardboard and Styrofoam filled his nostrils.

It made no sense. The artifact didn't look any different than it had at the museum, but it was obvious that something was burning the area around it.

Maybe it's switching on and off, but everything we were told said this thing was about messing with memories, not heating shit up.

Logan reached down to touch the circlet, and heat seared his fingertips. He jerked his hand back and shook it out.

"Why the fuck is it so hot? Did anyone do anything to it?"

Logan looked over his shoulder at his gathered men, and they all shrugged and shook their heads. He picked up the box and set it on the ground. Whatever was going on, he didn't trust that it wouldn't damage the van. They needed to get this shit under control.

He pulled out his phone and dialed Tak. Screw the video conferencing. The dwarf would have to deal.

"Tell me something useful," Tak answered. "I don't like my time being wasted."

Better lead with the shit he wants to hear. That'll make him less pissy about the other crap.

Logan rattled off the names of the hostages. "Any of those names mean anything to you? Just seem like guards and two random bitches to me. I don't see any reason to keep them alive."

"Hmm. No, those names are meaningless to me. They are expendable. Do whatever you feel is appropriate. Is that all?"

"No. Something weird is happening with the circlet."

Tak let out an annoyed grunt. "Weird? Care to be a bit more specific? It's a powerful magical artifact. 'Weird' could manifest in a lot of ways."

"It's hot as fuck all of a sudden. I tried to pick it up, and it burned my hand." The sting from the light burn lingered.

"I see." Tak offered a weary sigh. "Is it glowing? Has it changed colors? Is it shifting in and out of perceptible reality?"

Logan blinked. "No. Uh, not that I can tell."

"Is it making any noise? Talking?"

"Talking?"

Tak snorted. "I don't have time for you to be surprised. I just need you to answer the questions. Is it making any noise or talking?"

"Nope. Nothing like that." Logan glanced back at the circlet. "Just hot. It's burning the box and the packing peanuts. I'm kind of pissed, Tak. You told us we wouldn't need any special containment gear, and now I'm wondering if I'm gonna end up with cancer."

"You shouldn't have needed any special gear or arti-facts," the dwarf snapped. "I researched this extensively." He took a deep breath. "One moment. Let me check on something. Don't hang up if you value your fingers."

"Fine."

Logan rolled his eyes at the phone. He hated working for the dwarf, but he couldn't turn down the huge amount of money he'd offered.

Might as well take care of at least some of this shit while I'm waiting.

The criminal leader looked at his men and pointed with his free hand toward the hallway leading to the room where they were keeping the hostages. He made a throat-slicing gesture with his finger.

Should have just killed them all at the museum and saved ourselves the trouble.

One of the men nodded and jogged toward the room.

Logan peered at the circlet again, still surprised it wasn't glowing. The box was starting to smoke, and the Styrofoam peanuts were melting.

"Shit, we're gonna have to pull it out of that box before it starts a fucking fire."

"Leave," Tak shouted over the phone.

"What?" Logan responded, furrowing his brow in confusion. "Leave what?"

"Leave the warehouse right now, you imbecile. The heat. It's a tracking resonance. Someone with access to strong magic is closing on your location."

Logan gritted his teeth. "What the fuck?"

"If it's that hot, they are very, very close. Take the loss on the circlet. If you're moving, you can at least delay any other resonances until I can come up with a countermeasure. But move."

"Damn it," Logan shouted. "Everyone close up! Fucking leave, leave, leave! It's time for the backup plan. Remember, you don't stop for more than twenty fucking minutes."

The men scrambled toward their respective vans, throwing open the doors and piling in the front and the back.

The remaining thug pointed at the box with the circlet. "What about that? That's worth a lot of money."

"Leave it. His orders." Logan shook his head. "And money won't do us any good if some angry Oriceran artifact collector blows us up with a fireball."

He pulled out a remote and pressed a button. The grinding sound of metal echoed throughout the warehouse as the loading bay door started to rise.

I knew this shit was working out too well. Fuck.

Logan slammed the back doors shut on the van and hurried into the driver's seat. The last thug hopped inside, and he started the vehicle. The engines of all five vans hummed.

Tires screeched as the vans peeled out the now open loading bay door. As each van hit the street, they alternated directions and then split off further until each vehicle was taking a different route away from the warehouse.

Logan blew out a breath.

Too damned close, but with the circlet there and all the men gone, we'll be all right. No one will catch us. We've still got this.

He frowned. He felt like he was forgetting something, but what?

The thug glanced down the hallway over his shoulder as he made his way to the hostages. It had almost sounded like the vans were starting and people were shouting.

"Whatever. I'll kill them and then go check."

A thug whistled right outside the door, but Maria was far more concerned about the shouting and sounds of vehicles starting.

She frowned. "What the hell is all that noise? Wonder what's going on?"

"It's an opportunity to go to stage two of the plan." Shay stood. "This is our chance. I need you to help me though. I need a step. Even your leg will do. I won't have enough momentum in this tiny room to pull off what I'm planning otherwise, and without my hands I'm limited."

The AET lieutenant stared at the other woman, not comprehending what she wanted. After a moment, she nodded. Shay must have needed something she could kick off, and the cop could provide that.

We'll show that asshole why he shouldn't be whistling while he works.

Maria knelt on one knee, bringing her other knee parallel to the ground.

The door glowed, and the lock clicked.

The sound of something rumbling in the distance echoed through the hallways. Squealing tires came next.

Seriously? What the fuck is going on?

The door opened, and an armed and masked thug entered.

Shay charged toward Maria, and the tomb raider leapt onto the cop's leg and pushed off. She flew toward the wall and then kicked off that hard surface, turning in the air and clamping her legs around the thug's head. With a quick shift of her body and legs, the tomb raider provided a nice example of the principle of conservation of momentum as she twisted and snapped the man's neck.

Shit. It's like killer parkour.

Shay released the man's neck but landed on her knee against the hard floor with a grimace. Not smooth, but considering she'd just killed a man while handcuffed, her inelegance could be excused.

Maria arched an eyebrow. The conscious guards all stared at Shay, their mouths agape.

Shay kicked the gun under some boxes and rolled the guard's body with her feet until he was away from the door. "The question now is whether we make a break for it or we wait it out."

Maria nodded. "All that noise might be a rescue team."

"I don't know. I didn't hear any shooting." Shay frowned. If it were James, there was no way he wouldn't be shooting everyone in sight. "We should go check it out, I think."

One of the guards shook his head. "We can't leave. It's insane to go out there." He nodded to the unconscious wounded man. "And what about him? We can't carry him handcuffed."

The cop nodded. Leaving a wounded man behind didn't sit well with her. She looked at Shay.

The other woman frowned and shrugged. She obviously wasn't happy with the idea of waiting.

Woman of action, huh? Guess that's why you're with Brownstone.

Maria moved over to peek out the door. She didn't spot anyone.

"I'm not hearing anything."

Shay moved toward the door and listened for a moment. "Yeah, whatever just happened, it's over, one way or another." She shook her head. "Fuck it. We need to go. If that wounded wizard is gonna have any chance of surviving, he needs medical attention. I say you and I go, Maria, and we can call in reinforcements. There has to be a phone somewhere."

The tomb raider spun toward the dead man. She kicked his pockets with her boot and frowned.

"I guess it'd be too easy if he had one on him. Damn it."

Maria looked at the dead man and the frightened guards. "Okay, I'm with you. The rest of you stay here, and we'll go get help."

One of the guards looked like he wanted to object, but he looked away instead.

The women crept into the hallway, taking careful steps as they listened for any voices or movement. Even in the locked room, they had still heard the occasional echo of talking or doors being opened and closed. Now there was nothing but silence.

Shay smirked. "Maybe someone screwed up a sleep spell and they're all out."

Maria snorted. "We should be so lucky. What's the plan now? We're free, but we're still in these magic cuffs."

The tomb raider nodded in the direction of the loading bay. "I saw offices on the other side of the loading bay." She then nodded toward the end of the hall. "And all we have there is a fire-alarmed door. We go that way, we guarantee that if anyone's still here, they'll be alerted and find us. I'm a badass bitch, but I usually can use my hands. I don't think I can take a bunch of guys handcuffed without the element of surprise."

Maria frowned. "But what if they're still in the loading bay? We'll be walking right into them."

"That's a chance we'll have to take." Shay blew out a breath. "You with me or not, Maria?"

"This is fucking annoying as hell, but I'm with you."

The tomb raider chuckled. "Yeah, not exactly my idea of a fun girls' night either."

They continued down the hall, taking slow and quiet steps, but only the tick of the occasional wall clock greeted them.

Maria picked up the pace. "They're gone."

Shay nodded. "I think so, too."

They paused at the turn in the hallway leading to the main loading bay. Maria peeked around the corner and narrowed her eyes.

No men. No vans. The only thing there was the smoldering remains of what looked like it used to be a cardboard box and a pile of melted white goo. Light glinted off a silvery surface in the pile of goo and burned cardboard.

It took a few seconds for the cop to process the sight before her.

Maria looked back at Shay. "They took off but left the circlet. Maybe tried to melt it? I don't know what the hell happened."

"That's a lot of money to leave on the table, even if they have all the other artifacts. Something must have really spooked them. Maybe—"

Distant gunfire echoed around the loading bay, along with breaking glass. Both women ducked around the corner.

Maria gritted her teeth. "Shit, they spotted us."

Shay shook her head. "I don't think so. It sounded like it was coming from the outside."

A loud pop was followed by something thudding against the cement floor.

After a few more gunshots, Shay smirked.

"How good are you at recognizing weapons by sound, Maria?"

The cop shrugged. "Decent, I guess. Why?"

"Because I'm pretty damned sure that whoever is firing is using a .45." Shay sprinted around the corner. "And I know at least one man who loves using .45s."

Maria hesitated and then ran after the tomb raider. Shay's plans had gotten them this far without getting hurt. Might as well ride the crazy sisterhood into hell.

They rushed into the main loading bay. A thick metal door lay on the ground, torn off its hinges. The mystery of its removal was solved when James Brownstone stepped through the open doorway, gun in hand and a frown on face.

"Damn," Maria muttered. "He *is* good."

Her eyes widened as a familiar man walked in about five steps behind Brownstone. Tyler.

Shay and Maria jogged toward the two men.

"Maria, stop," the tomb raider called.

The cop skidded to a halt. "What's wrong?"

Shay took a few steps toward Brownstone.

"Where the fuck are they?" he growled. He looked back and forth, an inferno of hatred in his eyes.

Maria's stomach knotted at the anger seeping out of every pore of the man. She'd seen him that angry when he'd taken down King Pyro. He had the eyes of a man ready to kill.

Shay offered him a smile. "We're fine. We're not hurt. One of the guards got shot, but he's still alive."

Brownstone holstered his pistol and continued to jerk his head around, obviously searching for a target for his wrath. "But where the fuck are they? I have a few questions to ask them with my fists."

"Gone." Shay shrugged. "Something spooked them, and they left. They sent one guard to kill us, but I took him out already. He and the museum guards are in a storeroom at the end of that hall over there."

Brownstone stomped toward the hallway.

Shay sighed. "He's already dead, James. I snapped his neck."

The bounty hunter stopped and took several deep breaths. He unclenched his hands slowly and nodded. "Lucky for him. He got the easy way out."

Maria made her way over to Tyler. "Now this shit I didn't expect."

The bartender shrugged and rubbed the back of his neck. "Don't read too much into it. I need you. Without you, I don't know if the neutrality of the Black Sun will hold. This is really just an investment in my business."

The cop smirked. "If that's the story you want to tell yourself, fine by me. I'm just glad you came. I'd throw my arms around you, but, you know, handcuffs. And from the looks of it, magical handcuffs."

She turned around to show him.

"I think I can do something about that, at least." Tyler pulled out his phone and dialed someone. After a few seconds, he smiled. "Dannec. Do you have an easy way to get off magical handcuffs? Yes. No. No, it's nothing like that. Maria and Brownstone's girlfriend got caught up in that museum thing. Yeah. Yeah. Okay, thanks." He rattled off the address.

Maria chuckled. "What did he say? And how much is it going to cost? Not like that elf does anything for free."

"He'll be here in twenty minutes, and you let me worry about the cost."

Brownstone's murder mask slipped away, replaced by obvious relief, but he kept quiet.

Shay walked over to give him a kiss on the cheek. "How the hell did you two even find us?"

Tyler held out his hands. Maria hadn't noticed it before, but they were blistered and reddened. It looked like he'd burned them.

"Tracking artifact," Brownstone rumbled. "We tracked the circlet."

The other man nodded toward the remains of the burned box. "Guess it got hot on both ends."

The box continued to smolder, and Maria frowned at it. "That's not going to explode, is it?"

Tyler shrugged. "Maybe."

James waited, hands in his pocket, as Dannec finished his work. Not being able to smash in the faces of the kidnappers left him unsatisfied, but now he wanted to get the hell out of there.

A glow and ethereal music ended with a quick flick of Dannec's hand. The cuffs fell off Shay, Maria, and the guards, who'd been brought into the front room.

The elf frowned as LAPD, both normal and AET, stepped out of their vehicles and set up a perimeter around the warehouse.

Dannec nodded toward the circlet. "I'm guessing you used a tracking artifact that got hotter as you got closer?"

"Yeah," Tyler replied. "Lucky I didn't burn my damned hands off."

"That's not the best type of tracking magic to use for obvious reasons, especially with a powerful artifact like that, but I suppose it got the job done."

James grunted. "That's all I give a shit about. Gonna deactivate it and track the rest of the objects. I don't want these assholes getting away."

The Professor hadn't really explained how to shut it off. Maybe the elf knew.

The elf shook his head. "That's not going to work. Didn't whoever gave you the artifact tell you about that?"

The bounty hunter frowned. "What do you mean?"

Dannec sighed. "The greater the power of the magical artifact involved in the tracking resonance, the longer it'll take to reset. Given that you traced the circlet, it'll probably take several weeks before you can track another object with your artifact."

"Fucking Professor. He could have mentioned that." James scrubbed a hand over his face.

It doesn't matter. I can still find these guys. Just need to use Peyton, and maybe the Professor has something else.

Two AET officers had set up cones linked with police tape to keep anyone from touching the circlet. The proximity of the crucifix and the circlet had resulted in both being blisteringly hot. If they hadn't been in the middle of a cement warehouse floor, it would have started a fire.

James had moved the crucifix into the bed of his truck. It wasn't hot enough to melt through the metal. At least not yet.

Sergeant Weber rushed up to Maria. "We've almost got the perimeter totally locked down, Lieutenant, but there is no sign of any of the suspects in this area. I've put out an APB for the vans you described, but there are a lot of Andercarr vans in the county."

She nodded. "I'm guessing they were long gone by the time we called you anyway, but maybe we'll get lucky" She turned to Brownstone, Shay, and Tyler. "Look, I'll handle everything here. You guys can get out of here."

"Thanks," James rumbled, and walked away.

Shay fell in at his side.

"Me, too?" Tyler asked.

Maria offered him a soft smile. "I can paper over a lot of shit here, even the fact that we've got a body, but it'll be easier if you aren't around for the wrong guys to question. I'll talk to you later. You'll probably have to sign a few things."

The information broker nodded and hurried after Shay and James.

None of the trio spoke as they walked out of the loading bay and into the cool night air. Red and blue flashing lights killed any true darkness. Every once in a while a cop walked toward them and opened their mouth, but once they saw James, they gave him a polite nod and returned to what they were doing.

Good. Don't have it in me to be polite right now.

He fingered the amulet under his shirt. The only reason he hadn't bonded with it was that he hadn't gotten away from Tyler. He wasn't ready to trust a criminal information broker with that kind of secret.

Would Whispy Doom give me the ability to track their asses?

James, Tyler, and Shay loaded into the F-350. The information broker took a seat in the back.

"This shit isn't over," the bounty hunter growled. He started his truck.

Tyler frowned. "Shay and Maria are okay. Isn't that enough?"

The tomb raider offered him a savage grin over her shoulder. "Come on, Tyler, you know how James thinks. Do you really think this is over?"

Tyler snorted. "What would your priests have to say about revenge, Brownstone?"

"Father McCartney would get bored if he didn't have me confessing all the time." James shrugged as he pulled onto the street. "And this isn't just about revenge. I took a job from the Professor to recover those artifacts. The police have the circlet, so that's one of them, but the rest are still out there. If you want in, there's money to be made, even if you don't give a shit about vengeance."

Tyler chuckled and shook his head. "I'm tempted. I really am. I might not be the kind of guy who will blow up a building to get revenge, but I'm pissed at the assholes for grabbing Maria. Unless you really need me, I need to stay out of this one, though. I'm a neutral information broker, not a bounty hunter."

James shrugged. "Your call. I'll take you back to the Black Sun, and then Shay and I have to go figure out how to find the rest of the items."

"Don't get me wrong. When you find them, Brownstone, I hope you end them."

The bounty hunter narrowed his eyes and tightened his hands around the steering wheel. "Don't worry. They'll get what's fucking coming to them."

Maria sat at a table in a museum conference room with a briefcase in front of her. Several other police officers from AET and other units lined the table. The conversation with the Head of Security was going about as well as she'd expected.

I think I'd rather be a hostage again.

Spencer Preston sat at the head of the table, his fingers steepled. "I fail to see why we're even having this meeting, especially since you've yet to return the circlet. You have no right to keep that artifact."

Maria offered a tight smile. "It's evidence in part of an ongoing investigation. I can assure you it'll be returned once the investigation is completed."

The man scoffed. "This is ridiculous. We don't even want the police here. We don't need your help."

Maria glanced at the other police officer before barking a laugh. "Are you kidding me?"

"No. This was all the LAPD's fault anyway. Obviously." He sneered.

"Oh? How is it *obviously* our fault?"

Spencer pointed at her. "You were kidnapped during their raid. Your presence here probably encouraged them to do it. If you hadn't come poking your nose into things, none of this would have happened."

Maria let out a long sigh and opened the briefcase. She pulled out a huge stack of papers and shoved them his way.

The man's brow furrowed, and he looked down at the stack. "What's all this?"

"A report. Yeah, I was here the other day checking out your allegedly great security, and that's a detailed point-by-point list of every single problem with your procedures. Do you really want to go through them one by one?" Maria shrugged. "The fact that this place got hit and those artifacts were stolen proves in and of itself that your security was crap, and I, along with my consultant and your guards, are only alive because we got lucky."

Spencer lips pursed. "I'm sure the guards will testify to how you interfered with their duties."

Maria scratched her eyebrow. "Oh, you were planning to threaten them or something? Maybe bribe them? Too bad they all gave statements already." She nodded toward the papers. "Those are in there, too. A couple of them even talked about how they'd brought up some of the concerns that my investigation identified but their concerns were dismissed."

"All lies to cover up incompetence."

"Oh, wait, so now you're saying the guards who you hired and said were good security are incompetent?"

Spencer flicked his wrist. "This is all absurd. This is just the LAPD overextending their authority. I refuse to play along with this farce."

"Nope. I've already sent up a request for AET to take the lead on the protection of these artifacts, given the obviously enhanced threat these criminals represent. We'll be liaising with other units and departments, of course, but these criminals aren't petty thugs. These are dangerous, ruthless crooks, and you obviously can't handle them."

The man shook his head. "More trouble occurred from efforts to stop this last night than anything."

Maria narrowed her eyes. "And what's that supposed to mean?"

I wonder if douchebag is hiding something. Could this have been an inside job?

Spencer stood and pushed in his chair. "I've had enough of this. If you force your way in legally, there's little I can do, but you proved how useful police are last night, Lieutenant. Thanks for nothing."

The man spun on his heel and stormed out.

Maria whistled. "Somebody's mommy didn't love him enough."

That morning the Brownstone dining room served as a makeshift operations center. James and Shay sat at opposite ends of the table, phones in hand.

James frowned at his phone. "You're sure. Already? It hasn't even been a fucking day."

The informant on the other end of the line laughed. "Just telling you what I heard, Brownstone. I don't make the news. I just report to anyone who pays me. I got one last thing to tell you, though. A little bonus, because I was told to play nice with you over this."

"Bonus?"

The man laughed. "Yeah, word on the street is, the uptown Oricerans at the embassy know you're looking into this and they ain't happy, even though the shit being stolen makes them look bad. They don't want you near this. Just thought you should know."

"Thanks. Call me if you find out anything else." James hung up.

Shay looked up from her phone. "Any luck?"

"Several minor artifacts are already on the black market."

The tomb raider nodded. "Peyton just sent me a text saying that as well."

"Probably shit they don't care about." James frowned. "But it's stolen, and the Professor wants it found. Shit. I think. He didn't exactly give a huge number of details when we talked, and I was too focused on finding you to ask."

Shay shrugged. "Then ask him."

The bounty hunter nodded and dialed the Professor.

The older man answered on the first ring. "I under-stand you already located the circlet. Good job, lad."

"Yeah, but the cops have it. I wasn't about to try to take it from them."

The Professor laughed. "Nor would I ask you to. The point of hiring you was to make sure that the most dangerous of those artifacts didn't end up in the wrong hands. It was always my intention to give them back to the rightful owners once you recovered them and...handled any unfortunate dark forces involved in their theft."

"So you don't mind if I kill a few of the bastards along the way?"

"Let's just say that I'm a big believer in people bringing on their fates through their actions." A quiet chuckle followed.

James grunted. "Okay. You forgot to tell me that the tracking artifact would only be good for last night."

"I sensed that you were focused on a quick resolution. I didn't see the need to burden you with what appeared to be unnecessary details."

James considered his response for several seconds. He couldn't come up with a good reason to lie to Smite-Williams.

"I was pissed because Shay was at the museum when they raided it. They'd taken her."

"And is the lovely Miz Carson unharmed?" An unusual level of menace infused the Professor's tone.

The bounty hunter snorted. "Yeah, she's fine. She even killed one of the fuckers while she was in handcuffs."

"Ah, then you can *both* focus on recovering the artifacts." The regular cheeriness returned to the Professor's voice.

"Yeah, I guess, but I'm running out of ideas on how to track them quickly. I do know that some are hitting the black market. I've got a guy or two I'm gonna talk to about that."

James figured that job would be perfect for Tyler but didn't want to mention the man's name in case the disdain went both ways.

"I'm very glad to hear that," the Professor responded.

"Shay talked to a gnome contact of hers and he was able to confirm that the objects are all still in the general area, but they've got some sort of anti-tracking spell on them. He couldn't give her more info than that. He said they might be in motion." The bounty hunter frowned. "You got anything else that might help?"

The Professor sighed. "Alas, for several reasons, I don't have immediate access to anything else that would help you, especially if they've already implemented counter-spells, but I have confidence that between you and Miz Carson you'll be able to find the items. Is there anything else I can do to facilitate their recovery?"

"I've heard that the guys at the consulate aren't happy I'm on this job."

"Hmm. I see. I was wondering how that might play out, given what happened in court. There are so many political ramifications to consider when it comes to Oriceran matters." He chuckled. "You'd think they would have been happy at us solving one of their problems."

James' hand tightened around his phone. "Don't give a shit about any of that. I just want to make sure they don't fuck with me on this. This shit is personal because the fuckers grabbed Shay, and if the uptight assholes from the consulate don't want to get hurt, they better stay the fuck out of my way, or I'll do to them what I did to the Drow queen."

The Professor chuckled quietly. "Very well, then, James. I have a few strings I can pull. At the very least, I can ensure that the Oricerans attached to the consulate leave you alone."

"Thanks," James rumbled. "I should get back to finding those artifacts."

"Please do."

The bounty hunter hung up and shook his head.

Shay looked up from her phone. "What's wrong?"

"I wanted Heather to have a vacation, but I think it's time I called in some reinforcements for Peyton."

Yev paced back and forth in his consular office, a deep frown on his face. "I can't believe this."

Erai held up her hands in a placating gesture. "I don't understand why you're so upset."

The consul spun and stared at the woman. The other Light Elf had only been on Earth for a week, part of a reshuffling of some of the consulate staff. Her eager earnestness alternated between refreshing and insufferable.

Yev took a deep breath and dropped into his seat. "You are familiar with everything that has happened with James Brownstone, are you not?"

The female elf frowned and nodded. "I was fully briefed, but I was under the impression the issue was centered around preserving stability in the Drow situation. With Qu...with Laena no longer queen, why the enmity toward this James Brownstone?"

The consul sighed. "You don't yet understand the political implications. This James Brownstone is a dangerous element, and now he has reason to distrust not only the Drow but our entire consular presence here. The last thing we need is for him to be so close to such a sensitive matter." He shook his head. "Not only that, he takes savagery and barbarism to new heights. No wonder he was able to defeat Laena."

A light melody filled the air, and Yev blinked. He snapped once, and an image of the upper half of a smiling Light Elf winked into existence.

Yev's eyes widened. Not just any elf. Correk.

The consul smoothed his expression. "It's been a long time, Correk. Last time we talked in earnest, you were just another servant of the king, same as me. How you've moved up in the world. Both worlds, I suppose."

The other elf shrugged. "I'm still a servant of the king."

"But only one of us is the Fixer."

Erai blinked and slapped a hand over her mouth.

Correk chuckled. "You make it sound so impressive. It's mostly a huge and annoying responsibility."

"It comes with access to the rarest artifacts and spell books." Yev didn't bother to hide the jealousy in his voice.

"Which I use to protect the magical beings of Earth." Correk sighed. "Speaking of that, I have a favor I would ask of you."

Yev forced a smile. "I'd be more than happy to assist the Fixer."

"It's come to my attention that James Brownstone and Shay Carson are involved in a search for some stolen artifacts."

The consul's smile faded. "Shay Carson? I don't know who that is, but I'm well aware of Brownstone's involvement. I'm hoping to pressure the human authorities into removing him. He's too much of a disruptive element."

"I can't say I disagree with that assessment overall, but he also tends to get things done. I'd ask that you not fight his involvement with this, at the minimum. If he comes to you in need of protection, I'd like it to be offered as well."

"Well, if it's for the Fixer, I can hardly refuse, can I?"

Correk let out a quiet snort. "Everything I do is for the stability of all magical beings on Earth."

Yev forced his mouth into another smile. "So you do. I'll see to it that Brownstone's given our blessing, Fixer."

"That's all I can ask. Thank you for your assistance. Be well."

Yev nodded. With that, Correk's image faded. He turned to the wide-eyed Erai. "Make sure that the consulate staff knows we're extending our blessing to Brownstone's involvement in this as a personal favor for the Fixer."

Seems like I almost never come to this place anymore, James thought. *Am I wasting money by even keeping it?*

He carried a suitcase filled with weapons out of the storage unit into the hallway. It joined several others he'd already removed. He stepped back into the room and through the open door in the false wall that led to what properly constituted his warehouse.

It might not be as fancy as any of Shay's, but it'd gotten the job done for years.

Shelf after dusty shelf lay empty. Only a few suitcases remained. His gaze dipped to the secure safe that contained a smaller safe. The two used to form the resting place for his amulet, a secure and hidden place for a dangerous artifact, but now that he'd promised Alison to keep it on him, the safes seem pointless.

Wonder if Whispy Doom ever got annoyed that I kept him in there all the time? Not like he's mentioned it since I've been able to understand him.

He shook his head and grabbed another suitcase, one of

the few go bags he had left. Before, they'd made perfect sense. Now, he simply didn't care. He kept most of his equipment in his basement, and with the amulet always available, it dramatically decreased his risk going into any single encounter.

Might as well keep all my shit where I can get to it easily. At this point, it's not like the cops don't know I'm packing all my crap. Who am I hiding it from here? Bounties?

The bounty hunter carried the go bag into the hallway.

Shay leaned against a wall in the main unit, looking at her short nails. Mostly empty boxes filled the room. A few old truck parts lay around, just in case anyone ever broke in. He didn't want them wondering about why he was renting the unit, leaving a loose thread that begged to be pulled.

"Angels Elite Indoor Long-Term Storage," Shay muttered. "And this is what you call a warehouse? I can't believe my man would dare call this a warehouse. It's an insult to warehouses everywhere."

James hurried and grabbed another suitcase, this one filled with specialty electronics. Jammers of various sorts, mostly. He set it in the hallway.

He smirked. "Some of us don't need to compensate for anything with the size or number of our warehouses."

Shay winced and shook a fist. "Okay, that was a good hit, but give me some time, and I'll get you back, James Brownstone."

He retrieved one last suitcase and dropped it in the hallway with a grunt. Something metallic jostled inside.

Shay pointed at the suitcase. "What was in that one? More jammers?"

James shook his head. "Lots and lots of grenades. I was worried about keeping explosives in the house before with Alison, but, shit, I had her throw a few during the summer, and she's a teenager, not a toddler, as well as a Drow with powerful magic. Besides, she knows not to fuck around with them."

Shay laughed. "Yeah, I would have loved to have seen you talk about that in court." She lowered her voice. "Your Honor, I think my daughter should be allowed to handle live grenades. After all, she's a Drow princess and can probably fry your brain by snapping her fingers."

James grunted. "Handling weapons teaches responsibility. At least with weapons, people get that they are dangerous. With cars, any random teen gets to drive around tons of death, and people act like that makes all the sense in the world. Magic makes more sense than that shit."

"Don't talk to me about teens and responsibility. I was killing people when I was fifteen." Shay pointed to the suitcase. "Just saying, maybe treat your bag filled with grenades with a teensy bit more caution."

"Doing shit how I always do it, and I'm not dead yet."

"I guess it really is better to be lucky than good." Shay sauntered over to the false wall and peered inside. "This place is all but empty now. Nothing sadder than empty storage. It makes the whole thing feel pointless."

"What? Should I fill it up with random crap like you have in half of Warehouse Five?"

"It's not random crap. Well, it kind of is, but it has a point." Shay smirked. "I have that as camouflage. Just saying, this place is pretty damned empty. I'm surprised. It's been a while since I was here last."

"I don't come here much anymore." James patted his amulet. "The main reason I used to come was for Whispy Doom, and I keep him with me all the time now."

Shay pointed to one of the remaining boxes. "What's in the last few boxes?"

"Mementos. Some of the few I have left. Most of my shit went up in smoke when the fuckers blew up my first house." The bounty hunter shrugged. "But it's not like I can keep all my shit locked up, so most of the crap that I gave a fuck about that was here I've already brought to my new house. I've got a lot more people watching my back now, so I figure my house won't get blown up as easily."

Shay took one last look at the few boxes remaining in the hidden compartment. "Wonder what kind of mementos those are? Care to enlighten me?"

"You want to know?"

"Yeah."

"You'll find out someday." James grinned. "When I think you're ready."

Shay laughed. "You're such an asshole."

"Yeah. We agree on that." He nodded toward the hallway. "I've got more than enough shit here to keep us in asskicking for a week. Did you still want to grab something from one of your warehouses?"

"Yeah, a few things from Warehouses Three and Five. Might as well grab the *Masamune* just in case we run into some tougher magical defense. These guys do have magic, so we shouldn't assume we can just gun their asses down." She smiled. "And I figure if you can kill a Drow Queen with the sword, that should be good enough for anyone we will run into."

James grunted. "I defeated her, but I didn't kill her."

"Close enough." Shay blew out a breath as she stepped into the darkened hallway. "I'm ready to find these assholes and pay them back."

The bounty hunter's face tightened. "So am I. You thinking about getting Lily involved in this?"

Shay shook her head. "No. I'm training her to be a tomb raider, not a bounty hunter. This is gonna get bloodier than she needs to be around."

"You that thirsty for revenge?"

"Look, I don't even care that much that they tried to kill me. Lots of people try to kill me. I'm more embarrassed than anything."

James stared at her. "Embarrassed?"

"Yeah." Shay sighed. "I got caught in a wide-area sleep spell. I even saw it coming. It's fucking rookie shit. I've faced way worse than that on tomb raids. Hell, I would have laughed at Alison or Lily if it happened to them."

The bounty hunter shook his head. "But Alison can do magic, and Lily can see the future. Sometimes, at least."

"Still not an excuse." Shay snickered. "Don't worry, once we track these assholes down, I'll earn my pride back." She grabbed a suitcase. "Let's load up your truck and head to some real warehouses so I can remind you how it's done."

The driver tightened his hands around the wheel. "This is bullshit. I can't believe we're supposed to drive until the transfer."

Their abrupt fleeing of the warehouse on Logan's order

had left the man unsettled, and the fact he'd only gotten a few hours of sleep didn't help things.

His partner looked at him and shook his head. "Are you kidding me?"

"What?"

"You *did* hear who showed up right after we left the warehouse, right? Fucking Brownstone, then the AET. If he didn't kill us, they would have arrested our asses."

The driver changed lanes. "Just saying. We were supposed to grab the shit and sit in that warehouse, but now we're driving all over L.A."

"The more we move, the harder it is for them to track us. Stick to the plan; no more than twenty-minute stops or shorter. We took too long the other day when we transferred some of the cargo to the other van."

The driver ground his teeth. "I should have known this job was gonna go south. I could smell it. Ain't no such thing as an easy job. We've gotten too cocky with this shit."

His partner snorted. "It doesn't have to be an easy job, it just has to be worth doing."

A few minutes passed in tense silence until the driver pulled into a gas station.

"What are you doing?" his partner asked. "You've got plenty of gas."

"I've got to take a leak."

The other man frowned. "But we've got a transfer schedule. We need to be on time. Logan or Tak don't like guys who don't do what they're told."

The driver threw open the door and stepped outside. "I said I have to take a fucking leak."

"We need to get going."

"I ain't driving with piss down my leg!" The driver flipped him off.

Tyler rested his elbow on the bar as he scrolled through his texts. Word had gotten out that he'd shown up with Brownstone at a warehouse. A few people had accused him of being a sellout to the police. Others wanted to know if another betting pool was coming.

Fuck. How did shit get so complicated? Did I just screw myself over?

Tyler had never thought of himself as a man who took sides. In fact, he'd prided himself on being able to make money off any situation. Loyalty was for suckers. It wasn't profitable.

I wasn't helping Brownstone anyway. I was helping Maria.

He scrubbed a hand over his face and sighed.

Kathy approached the bar, a tray of empty glasses in hand. "Problem?"

"Nothing's wrong. Just tired."

She smirked. "There are worse things in life than people thinking you're a scumbag who might sell them out at the drop of a hat."

Tyler frowned at her for a moment, more concerned about how she had so effortlessly picked up on what he was thinking than the lack of respect for her boss.

He set his phone on the bar. "This place can't function unless it's neutral ground."

Kathy stepped behind the bar and set the tray down. "Sure. *This* place. Not the city."

133

"What do you mean?"

The brunette gestured at different customers. A pair of huge bikers sat in one corner. Surprisingly, they were downing pink strawberry daiquiris. Three obvious triad members held down another corner. A group of gang-bangers had taken over most of the front tables. Several business jerks and obvious tourists filled the rest of the place, their faces showing how excited they were to be around so many rough characters.

Tyler shrugged. "I still don't get your point."

"Cops don't arrest anyone who comes in. Crooks don't start crap." She crossed her arms. "You've got a good business going just from the bar now. Doesn't matter if you're an official information broker, you're going to hear things."

He nodded toward the bikers. "What do you think those guys would do to me if they thought I had given them up to Brownstone?"

Kathy laughed. "Brownstone? I think they wouldn't do shit."

"Huh?"

"The guy's dog dies, he takes out houses filled with people. His girlfriend gets grabbed, he rushes across the city to kill whoever dared to do it." Kathy leaned against the bar and shrugged. "You might be Brownstone's bitch, but he's the damned Scourge of Harriken. Being associated with him isn't such a bad thing."

Tyler sighed. "Don't know."

A rough-looking elf sat down at the end of the bar.

Kathy started toward him before winking over her shoulder. "Just saying, if you've gotta pick a side, you might as well pick the winning one. I think you know who wins whenever someone goes up against Brownstone."

Tyler rubbed his chin as he considered that. A moment later the door opened, and Maria strode inside in full uniform.

Fuck. Talk about things getting complicated

The AET lieutenant marched up to the bar and jumped on a stool. "I'm off-duty, so give me something decent."

Tyler chuckled and grabbed some vodka. "How about a White Russian?"

Maria shrugged. "Fine by me."

The bartender started mixing the drink. "Everything going okay?"

"So far. We're still tracking the thieves, but at least nailing down the circlet has the brass satisfied. The consulate was making noise about being unhappy that Brownstone was attached to all of this, but they suddenly did a one-eighty."

Tyler finished mixing the drink and set it in front of the woman. "They did?"

"Yeah. First, they're all, 'He's a disruptive element who probably harbors a bias against Oricerans, and we don't want him involved in the recovery of the artifacts.'"

The bartender snorted. "Brownstone is racist against Oricerans? He adopted a half-elf girl. He's taken down more wizards and witches than Oricerans."

Maria shrugged. "That's just what they said, but then not that many hours later, they contacted the police chief and expressed their full support for Brownstone being involved. They even said that if he needed extra resources, they could look into it. Don't know. Politics is above my pay grade and gives me a headache."

Tyler chuckled. "Humans, elves, gnomes, witches… It's all the same shit in the end. Everyone's trying to put one over on everyone else." His smile drifted away, and he sighed. "Without Brownstone's contact lending him that artifact, I don't think we would have gotten there in time."

"Yeah, from what we can figure, they probably got spooked by the circlet getting hot and knew you guys were coming." Maria smiled at Tyler. "I came here about that, by the way."

"What do you mean?"

Maria picked up her drink and took a sip. "I wanted to give you a personal thank you without being distracted by police shit."

Tyler waved a hand dismissively. "It's no big deal. Shit, if I'm honest—and it annoys me to admit this—Brownstone did the heavy lifting. I mean, not like I didn't do anything. He got the artifact, but then I got the intel that you guys were somewhere in Koreatown. It's no big deal. He did all the kicking-down-doors shit." He shrugged. "And like I told you, I need you to help enforce the Black Sun's neutrality. If you died, the next AET lieutenant might not be so keen on supporting a guy like me."

The woman gulped down half her drink and let out a long breath before leaning in. "Look, I know what it takes to go into a situation where you don't know what's going on or the kind of danger you might face. I even know what it's like to go in behind James Brownstone, and when I do that, I've got armor, a whole tactical team, and a pile of fancy toys to protect me."

Tyler stared into the woman's dark eyes, unsure what to say.

Maria grinned. "Your nuts must have been playing footsie with your tonsils. But we're not kids. We should be real about this shit. I like you, and I know you like me. And I don't like you because I think you're the kind of guy who'll kick down doors and charge into a warehouse to save me." She looked around a bit before leaning over the bar and closer to Tyler. "But the fact that you showed up there with a gun? Not going to lie. It was an unexpected aphrodisiac."

Tyler opened his mouth to offer a retort or at least a response, but "Uh…" was all he managed.

The cop grinned and threw back the rest of her drink. "I'll be seeing you again soon, Tyler." She winked. "All of you."

Maria set her glass and rose. She headed toward the front door, swaying her hips as she went.

Kathy walked back over from serving the elf. She patted Tyler on the shoulder.

"You are so screwed, and I mean that figuratively." The brunette nodded toward the departing Maria. "And as soon as she can manage it, literally."

Tak leaned back in the chair in his office and took a long, deep breath. The Council wouldn't want excuses. They would want results, or at least the promise of results.

It doesn't matter. Everything is still proceeding well enough. We all knew there would be some losses along the way in this operation. Their cause can't be achieved without the occasional setback. They aren't naïve enough to believe otherwise.

He couldn't stall any longer. They were expecting a report, and the longer he waited, the more annoyed they'd be.

The dwarf retrieved a small coin inscribed with glyphs and set it atop a flat wooden disk. A pulsating circle of light surrounded the disc, and a low hum filled the air.

A few seconds later, six hooded and robed figures appeared in front of him. He'd almost believe they were here if he didn't know better. The fact that they weren't allowed him some small comfort.

If I knew who they were, would I even care, as long as they kept rewarding me?

"Report," barked one of the figures. Even without seeing the face Tak could tell it was a male, probably an elf of some sort.

The dwarf could never be sure who was in charge. Even though it always seemed like the same six people, it wasn't always the same individuals in control of the conversation.

Of course, it might not be the same six. It'd be easy enough to fake a voice and general size, especially via this remote link. They obviously all have powerful magic.

Tak cleared his throat. "The project is proceeding per your instructions, but there have been some complications. That said, we are still well within the margin of error, and I don't anticipate any issues with the overall completion of your goals."

Another figure stepped forward. "Complications? Elaborate."

This time the voice was feminine but husky.

"The authorities were able to track my team to the first location before the vans split up. One of the men was killed on site, but he was disposable, so that's not that important."

Several of the robed figures exchanged looks, their faces still hidden from Tak.

A shorter figure stepped forward. A dwarf or gnome, perhaps.

Could I end up on this Council someday if I prove my resourcefulness and loyalty?

"Any artifact losses?" the short figure inquired.

Tak nodded. "The authorities have the circlet. My men were forced to abandon it."

"Why would you abandon the circlet?"

The dwarf shrugged. "There was a heat-resonance tracking spell being used that made it clear the circlet was being followed."

The short figure took a deep breath. "Unfortunate. We wished to study the circlet. Its abilities would have been useful for our plans."

"I understand that, but I was also told that a loss of any single artifact was well within the parameters of this operation."

The shorter figure shook his head. "I hope for your sake that this remains a single lost artifact."

The first speaker spoke next. "That was the only loss thus far?"

Tak nodded. "Yes, the rest of the artifacts were successfully evacuated, and with the authorities distracted, further anti-tracking magic was implemented. The minor artifacts, per your instructions, are already being disposed of in the local black market. The van that was carrying them is being used as a decoy."

The tall robed figure nodded. "The circlet is an unfortunate loss, but we will tolerate it—provided there are no further mistakes. The authorities don't realize the importance of everything you've taken. Perhaps leaving the circlet behind will reinforce that erroneous idea." He shook a dark-gloved finger. "But remember, Tak, when you serve the Council you earn great rewards if you please us, and agony if you displease us. Rhazdon was weak and short-sighted compared to us."

Oh, please. Do you think you scare me with Atlantean boogeymen? Such threats are beneath both of us.

Tak kept a slight smile on his face. They wanted his fear, but he wouldn't give it to them. He didn't care about whatever inscrutable plans the Council had. The only thing that mattered to him was that they provided the rewards promised for completed jobs.

"I've taken on several jobs for you in the past," the dwarf offered, "and I've never failed you. I won't fail you this time either. I will do what is needed and make the necessary sacrifices." He held up four fingers. "There are four remaining vans with artifacts. Four clients. Everything's proceeding as you ordered. Everything's been transferred and consolidated. One contains generic artifacts to be sold for more funding, a second carries the artwork artifacts, a third has the artifacts for research, and the last will go into your vault. My men are implementing a plan to avoid being tracked." He gave them a defiant stare. "I presume this meets with your approval?"

"You are following directions well," the tall figure replied. "We'll grant you that, but there are still plenty of opportunities for the authorities to track you."

Tak shook his head. "The authorities had their one good chance at the warehouse, and they only managed to get the circlet. I won't fail the Council, I promise you that. I know the price of failure."

The hooded figures all nodded.

Another figure moved forward smoothly, as if gliding forward rather than taking steps. Even the outline of the robe around its body was unnatural and too stiff.

"See that you don't," rasped the figure, its voice hollow. "Or I'll be coming to visit you."

Heather rolled into the living room. Her son Noah closed the door behind her. He dragged in a small rolling suitcase before locking the door.

The woman sighed. It was hard to even look at her little cherub's face without feeling guilty. "I'm sorry, sweetie, that I couldn't just share one more day with you. All that fun and sun. I know I promised a whole week, and... I'm just so sorry."

Noah shook his head. "It's okay, Mommy." He walked over and pulled her into a hug. "I love you, Mommy. We got to play a lot."

She offered him a bright smile. "I have to work tonight, but we can put on some cartoons and eat pizza. You just think about what sort of pizza you'd like. I'll order any kind you want."

He cheered. "Yay! I want Hawaiian."

"Sure, sweetie. We can order a large Hawaiian, and I'll order pop for you, too."

"Yay." Noah clapped his hands together.

"Why don't you take your suitcase to your room? You can pull out those Disney pajamas we got and wear them later."

Her son bounced a few times. Heather sighed again as Noah scurried to his room with a happy look on his face.

I hate that I have to do this to him, but helping James is the only chance we have for a real future in which we don't have to be afraid anymore. I know he wouldn't have called me back in if he didn't have a good reason.

Or is that just what I'm telling myself to feel better?

Heather shook her head and rolled into her bedroom. She would make it up to Noah, but she needed to take care of business first. She pulled out her phone and called James.

"Hey," the bounty hunter rumbled. "You back in town? Or, shit, guess you could have helped from anywhere."

Heather sighed. "No, not really. Sure, I have the skills to do it, but I don't want to be doing work while in a hotel room with shitty Wi-Fi, let alone around my son."

"Fuck. I'm really sorry about this."

"It's okay. You don't decide when criminals do what they do. Well, you did with Lars Hansen, but *usually,* you don't decide."

James grunted.

Heather allowed herself a chuckle. "Anyway, I just got back. I haven't had a chance to check on anything about the museum yet, but I'll hit the ground running tonight."

"Good to hear. Really gonna need your help with this shit."

"Is there anything in particular you want me to focus on?" She rolled over to her computer and moved the mouse. The screen lit up.

"There were five vans at the warehouse," James replied. "They were disguised as Andercarr delivery vans, but I have no fucking clue if the assholes have changed that since people saw them at the warehouse. The LAPD's got drones flying around, but it's not like they can stop every single delivery van out there. Do what you can to help track them down first. They hacked the surveillance system at the museum so it might help you to look into that. You know better than I do how to look into shit using computers."

Heather cradled the phone between her shoulder and cheek as she started typing. "Need any active drone support?"

"Nope, not really. I've got Shay with me, so I'll have someone guarding my back."

The hacker clucked her tongue. "Working with your girlfriend. Don't know if it's a good idea."

"It's fine. Shay and I share the same philosophy on beating people down. Oh, yeah, that reminds me. Just so you know, Peyton will be working this job soon. Is that gonna be a problem?"

"Nope." Heather chuckled. "If anything, it's good."

"Good?" James asked.

"Yeah. This will let me prove who the better hacker is."

The wizard smiled as he looked out the window.

The sun hung low in the sky. It'd be setting soon. Even if the building lights and signs made sure it was never truly dark in Los Angeles, a little extra cover would help disrupt the authorities' attempts to track them.

The wizard tried to push the lingering fear out of his head. Word was that James Brownstone might be involved with tracking the artifacts.

What do I care if Brownstone is involved? He's a bounty hunter, not some bloodhound or a god. Last few major show-downs involved people coming to him. There's no way he'll track us down, not with the magic anti-tracking we have now.

The man licked his lips, his heart pounding. He needed to concentrate on his immediate task and get things ready for the next artifact transfer.

Fuck Brownstone. He hasn't dealt with an organization like us before.

The SUV sped toward a highway tunnel, traffic dense around it. Most people would have been annoyed to have driven into rush-hour traffic, but the driver of the SUV couldn't stop grinning. Everything was going according to plan.

Yeah, just follow the plan, and soon we'll be safe and away from Brownstone.

The wizard reached underneath his jacket and pulled out his wand. "We're almost there. This is going to go quickly once I start. Make sure you're paying attention, so you don't kill us."

"I know how to avoid accidents." The driver snorted. "Just give me a countdown. That way I'm not surprised, and you don't got nothing to worry about. Just do your thing, Harry Potter, and let me do mine."

"Fuck you. Call me that again, and I'll use this wand on your dick."

The driver grinned. "Make sure the guys in the van are still ready. You're sure about that spell behind us?"

"Yeah. It won't last long, but it'll last long enough." The wizard glanced down at the phone in the console and the last text.

Closing on the tunnel. Get ready

"They haven't sent another message," he announced.

The driver nodded. "Then make a little magic happen, baby."

"Five," the wizard began, "four, three, two, one."

Time to make a distraction.

The driver jerked the wheel hard to the side. The wizard raised his wand and muttered an incantation, and a bright flash lit the darkened tunnel. Five cars ahead of them, the very unfortunate driver of a sedan suddenly had to contend with two simultaneous blowouts.

Tires screeching and rims sparking, the sedan swerved, and the driver of the pickup behind the car slammed on his brakes.

Too damned slow. The vehicles collided, and several more cars behind the wizard's SUV hit their brakes as well. The hideous crunching of metal echoed through the tunnels. Debris shot up and around, some colliding with the tunnel roof and sparking.

Shit. That worked better than I'd planned.

The two men gritted their teeth as a car slammed into them from behind. The briefest blue flash revealed the protection spell cast over the SUV. More and more cars stopped.

A shower of debris fell as traffic ground to a halt.

The wizard opened the window and looked both ways. With a truck and multiple cars on their side in front of them, no one would be getting through the tunnel anytime soon, and with all the cars behind them, the police and wrecker responses would be slowed.

He grinned. His phone chimed with a text.

Good job. We're about 10 cars back. See you soon

15

P eyton rubbed the back of his neck as he stared at his screen. Long-range drone footage had helped him spot the five vans as they'd initially departed, but he'd lost them after that. His search of the dark web had helped him locate the items on the black market, and he'd passed that information on to the Professor directly at Shay's request.

Apparently, the old man was more than content to pass that information to the LAPD and let them handle it while James and Shay went after the other targets. The job was about keeping the artifacts off the street rather than delivering them to the Professor.

"Come on, you sons of bitches, where are you?" the hacker mumbled.

Their use of plate protectors made any attempt to pull their license plate numbers from a distance pointless, but it did raise the chance that some local cop might pull them over. Peyton didn't believe he'd have that luck, so he needed to make his own.

A notice popped up on his screen, and he clicked on it. A grin spread across this face.

"Yeah, you guys thought you were so clever, but you forgot you were dealing with me." He shook his head. "It's almost unfair that you had to go up against me."

Peyton had set up a few bots to monitor traffic drones and cameras for vans meeting the general description of the ones from the warehouse. Typically, he'd also have the bots try to process images and pull license plates numbers. In this case, he did the opposite. He looked exclusively for vehicles where the license's plate *couldn't* be read.

The hacker typed in a few commands and brought up a series of video feeds from hacked cameras and drones. After a couple of minutes of fast-forwarding through the feeds, he frowned.

"The guy's not going anywhere fast. Is he lost?"

Peyton scratched his cheek and considered his prey. Maybe he was wrong. He doubted that a group of professional thieves would be so ill-prepared as to get lost, but he'd found a vehicle that seemed to be driving in erratic circles.

He snapped "Shit. Unless they have to keep moving until some rendezvous?"

LA was huge. Even with all the cameras and drones, it was hard to track everyone and everything, especially if they were on the move.

Peyton leaned forward and entered a series of commands. He needed more information. There had to be something in the area that might tip him off where the van might be going, or even if it were truly one of the thieves' vans.

A Highway Patrol alert popped up.

Multi-car traffic accident at Sepulveda Boulevard Tunnel. Traffic is at a standstill. Please use alternate routes.

Peyton frowned. The van had been staying pretty damned close, at least in LA terms, to the tunnel, and it didn't help his suspicions that the tunnel ran under the LAX runways.

Quick getaway in a private plane, maybe? Or just a coincidence?

Another alarm popped up. His bots had located another van.

Oh, it's almost criminal to be this good.

He picked up his phone and dialed Brownstone.

"What do you got?" the bounty hunter rumbled.

"Major traffic accident in the Sepulveda Boulevard Tunnel." Peyton clicked through video feeds until he found a traffic drone. A little searching yielded the van. "And one of the vans drove into that tunnel, but you've got another likely candidate only a few miles from you." He rattled off the intersection.

James grunted. "We'll hit the closer assholes, first. The other guys are bottled up, it sounds like."

The driver of the van smiled as the two wreckers made their way through traffic. He had to hand it to the Highway Patrol. They were going to get traffic moving again even quicker than they'd planned. After the warehouse fiasco, it was nice for something to work in their favor.

The thieves' vehicle sat in a long line of stopped cars in the darkened tunnel. No one was bothering to try to be clever and wedge their way in. Right now, everyone was probably staring at their phones, just waiting for traffic to move.

"It's funny," he commented to his partner. "Tons of cops here, and no one's noticed us."

"They're focused on the accident." The man in the passenger's seat shrugged. "But that doesn't mean they won't."

The driver shook his head. "Doesn't matter. We'll take care of them if they do. We both know what Logan will do to us if we lose this cargo. Besides, we can take on a bunch of Highway Patrol cops. It's not like they're AET."

His phone chimed.

They are about to move the first car. Looks like traffic's going to start moving. Get your asses up here before the plan gets totally fucked.

"Time to go." The driver grinned and pulled the van off on the shoulder. He turned it off and hopped out.

Both men rushed around to the back and threw open the doors. They grabbed the four laden leather bags from the cargo area before slamming the doors closed and locking the van. Might as well make it as annoying as possible for the police.

They rushed into the tunnel, almost no one paying them any attention. A half-minute of hard running brought the men to the SUV. The back hatch started rising as they approached. They darted along the shoulder and between a few cars.

The men threw the bags in and rushed to the opposite sides of the SUV as the back hatch started to close. They hopped into the back seat.

The new arrivals shared smiles with the driver and the wizard sitting in the passenger seat.

The wizard nodded forward. "Looks like traffic's starting to move."

The driver of the SUV smiled. "This is the easiest job we've had in a while."

Maria frowned at Sergeant Weber. "You're serious? We've got a sale location for several of the artifacts?"

Their operations command center was filled with officers and support staff tapping away on laptops or answering phones, all sitting or standing around a long black table. A corkboard with pictures of the artifacts hung on the wall, along with a map with several pins indicating possible sightings of the vans.

Weber nodded. "Yeah, an anonymous tip came in about artifact sales related to the robbery, and Major Crimes and Vice have both verified the location as being Russian Mafia-controlled. Handover is happening in about thirty minutes."

"Finally, some good luck for a change." The lieutenant frowned. "Do we know anything about the artifacts being handed over?"

Weber nodded. "Based on what the tip and what we've been able to pick up from informants, they're all stuff we classified as minor threats. Not all the minor stuff, but a lot of it."

"Get a small team together and liaise with Major Crimes and Vice. We'll raid some mafia asses. I want most of our manpower still on reserve." Maria shook her head. "We got the circlet, but there are still a lot of nasty artifacts out there we need to retrieve."

Matthews, who'd been talking on the phone, set the phone down and rushed over to Maria.

"We've got some major hits on the vans."

This is falling into place. We can catch these bastards.

"Other than the black-market deal?" she asked.

Matthews nodded. "Highway Patrol was cleaning up after an accident at the Sepulveda Boulevard Tunnel. Found an abandoned van there. Nothing inside."

Maria slammed her fist on the table. "Damn it. They switched vehicles? Anyone see anything?"

"We're checking any drones that went into the tunnel to find out if they saw anything." Matthews shrugged.

"So that's one out of five. Tell me you have some good news, too."

Matthews grinned. "Yeah, got two pieces of good news, maybe even three depending on how you look at it. We've got eyes on two of the other vans. They aren't together, though. Drones following them both. The first van's in Little Armenia right now. It's parked, but no one's gotten out."

Maria sighed. "Damn it. They're about to do a transfer

154

or move the artifacts." Maria pointed at Weber. "Get us some helicopters. Now."

The sergeant nodded once and rushed over to an open phone at the other end of the table.

"The second one's in Crenshaw," Matthews continued. "Drone also tagged an old F-350 not far behind the van. Plates say it's registered to one James Brownstone." He smirked.

The lieutenant grinned back at him. "Fine. We'll let him handle them, and we'll head after the second van with the rest of the team. We've got to nail these bastards."

She pulled out her phone to give Brownstone a call.

The driver of the third van, Trevor, glanced into his mirror and grimaced. Even in the early evening darkness, it was hard to miss the large truck following them. "Shit."

His partner Doug looked at him. "What?"

"How often do you see an F-350 anymore? They're practically antiques."

"What the fuck are you talking about?"

Trevor shook his head. "You know who drives an F-350, don't you? Fucking Brownstone."

Doug shrugged. "So what? With the artifacts Logan gave us, we can kick Brownstone's ass."

"You think so?"

"Yeah, I know so."

He reached into his pocket and pulled out a small golden needle. Gritting his teeth, he shoved it into his wrist and started intoning the Enochian incantation he'd been forced to memorize so many months earlier. He gagged and convulsed, straining against his seatbelt, arcs of red and black energy shooting across his body.

The driver winced. Trevor had seen it several times, but it didn't get any easier. "Don't die yet. You have to at least take out Brownstone first. I don't think I can shake him. I'm going to try, but the guy's like a fucking bulldog who just won't let go."

The other man opened his now-black eyes. "The only one who is going to die is Brownstone," he offered, his voice deeper.

James slipped his phone back into his pocket and accelerated.

Shay glanced at him. "I take it that was the cops?"

He nodded. "It was Hall. She says they are going after another van. She just told me, 'Good luck.'"

"Okay, we should be able to take one van of guys easily enough."

Kill the enemy, the amulet all but shouted in James' head.

Yeah, yeah. We'll get to that. Just let me fucking concentrate, asshole.

Kill the enemy. Become stronger.

Shay had insisted he bond with the amulet before they chased down anyone else. She'd been pissed when she found out that he'd not been using it during the warehouse raid.

James pushed his foot down, and the engine of his truck roared as he closed on the van. The other vehicle jerked to the side, almost colliding with another car as it rushed over to an exit.

He pulled hard on the wheel, heading into the exit after the vehicle. "I'll keep us on them. You do something to stop them. I doubt the cops will give us too much shit if the guys end up dead at the end of this, and the Professor doesn't seem to care as long as we get the artifacts or the cops do."

Shay rolled down her window and shook her head. "I hate car chases. I almost never needed a car chase when I was a killer. They're annoying as shit most of the time."

The bounty hunter grunted. "I have them all the time. Fuckers love to run."

"That's because you don't do a good job of surprising people." She rolled her eyes before she opened up with her 9mm. Bullets punctured the back of the van and sparked off the metal.

The van swerved and Shay shot several more times, but the target vehicle's quick movements saved it from serious damage.

Big mistake, assholes.

James grinned. Evasive movements were great for not getting hit, but shit for speed. He floored it, and the F-350 charged right at the swerving van.

Shay brought her hand back inside and gritted her teeth.

The truck crashed into the back of the other vehicle mid-swerve. The van overturned, scraping the road and leaving a trail of glass, metal, and plastic.

James kept a tight grip on the steering wheel as he rode the brakes and turned into his slide. He lost a few layers of rubber, but in the end, the F-350 didn't roll over or crash.

"Nice." Shay whistled. "Well, that shit was a lot easier than I thought. Guess not every fight has to be like taking on a Drow queen."

The wrecked van lay on its side. Half of the body was crumpled in. The door facing the sky ripped off the hinges and flew a good twenty feet into the air.

Strong enemy, the amulet whispered. *Destroy. Kill.*

"What the fuck?" Shay asked, and frowned.

The door crashed to the ground as a man in an Andercarr delivery uniform crawled out. He had no obvious weapons on him. A moment later, another man crawled out, also with no weapon.

James chuckled. "Got to give these guys credit; they're pretty damned tough. Looks like they're ready to give up. Not even gonna shoot at us. You're right, Shay. This shit is gonna be easy."

Kill the enemy. Defeat all enemies, the amulet whispered.

I already defeated them. They're about to give up.

Kill the enemy.

Fuck you. You don't tell me what to do.

The bounty hunter threw open his door and stepped out of his truck, his .45 out and ready. Just because the men didn't have obvious weapons didn't mean they weren't hiding something.

Shay hopped out the other side, her gun also at the ready.

"Get on your knees and put your hands behind your fucking heads if you want to fucking live," James bellowed.

"The only reason I'm not wasting your asses right now is that you haven't shot at me yet."

He frowned. It was hard to spot in the darkness, especially with only a few street lights nearby and the glow from a gas station down the road, but a semi-translucent red field surrounded one of the men. The other man's eyes were glowing bright blue. After a second, James realized the first man's eyes were solid black.

"Guess that explains why they didn't have any weapons," James muttered. "Should have known it wouldn't be that easy."

Sample unidentified threats, then kill, the amulet replied in his mind.

"My name's Trevor," Blue Eyes offered.

"And I'm Doug," the other man commented.

"I'm James Brownstone." He shrugged. "I don't give a fuck about your names. Get on your knees, or this is gonna hurt a lot. You assholes kidnapped someone you shouldn't have, and now I'm in a bad mood."

Shay groaned and rolled her eyes.

Sample, then kill, the amulet yelled in James' mind.

Shut the fuck up.

Trevor grinned. "We just wanted you to know the names of the men who are going to kill you, Brownstone. Don't worry, we'll make it quick."

The bounty hunter grunted. "That supposed to be scary, asshole?"

"Damn it, James," Shay shouted. "I swear, the minute some guy shows up and starts saying anything, it's like you want to have a shit-talking contest. Let's just be efficient about this crap for once."

The tomb raider opened fire at Trevor, but the bullets vanished in blue flashes.

Kill, kill, kill.

"Whatever," James muttered. He opened fire at the other man. Doug jerked with each hit, but his wounds closed almost instantly.

James and Shay kept firing until their guns clicked open. They swapped their mags.

The bounty hunter grunted. "You're tougher than I thought."

Trevor snorted. "Our turn." He nodded to Doug. "You take the bitch. I'll take Brownstone."

Both men yelled and charged.

James sighed, holstered his pistol, and rushed toward Trevor.

Doug opened his mouth. An unearthly scream erupted, along with a blast of black flame. Shay leapt to the side, and the flame exploded behind her. The force almost knocked her off her feet.

"That's national-level magic shit right there," the tomb raider shouted as she spun to avoid another blast.

Distracted by Shay getting attacked, James didn't see Trevor's fist coming. A heavy thud sounded, and the bounty hunter smashed into the ground a few yards away.

That was like getting nailed by a truck.

Trevor grinned and smacked a fist into his palm. "The great James Brownstone. Not really impressive in the end, are you?"

James stood up and moved his sore jaw back and forth. "You didn't break anything, asshole. Got to take me out before you can say that kind of shit."

Doug's echoing shrieks mixed with the sound of Shay's gun blasting away at him.

Maybe time to try something a little different. Gun's not working anyway.

James lifted his hand to focus his telekinesis. He attempted to jerk Trevor's legs out from under him, but nothing happened.

The other man snorted. "What's that supposed to do? Freak me out? I'm so scared."

What the fuck? Is he immune to it?

Ability not used, the amulet explained in his mind. *Core changed. Skin stronger.*

Are you fucking seriously saying you got rid of telekinesis because I didn't use it enough?

Yes. Skin stronger.

Can you bring it back?

Yes. If partner changes strategy.

James didn't know whether he should be furious or intrigued. Apparently, even his damn amulet had tactical revision notes for him now, but he did like the sound of "skin stronger."

"Pay attention to me, fucker!" Trevor shouted. "I'm gonna fucking end you."

The bounty hunter snorted. "Oh, yeah. You're still here."

He shook his head and rushed toward Trevor. The bounty hunter threw up an arm to block the other man's punch and slammed his fist into the criminal's head. The man jerked back but didn't go flying. James had to give him credit for that.

The two traded a flurry of blows. Trevor managed to get in a few decent hits, but they didn't do much more than sting. A powerful right hook from James and a punch into the stomach had the criminal staggering back, blood spraying from his mouth.

No use for adaptation, the amulet whispered. *Kill the enemy.*

Shay rolled, ducked, and dodged as Doug kept vomiting hellfire at her. She tossed a sonic grenade at him, but the man made no effort to dodge and didn't even seem to notice. Only the nearly ear-shattering whine let her know it had gone off.

James wanted to help her, but he needed to finish off the asshole in front of him first.

The bounty hunter smirked. "Thought you were gonna kill me, asshole."

Trevor wiped some blood off his face. "You're nothing, Brownstone. Maybe I should tell Doug to back off so we can have a little fun with the bitch over there after I kill you."

James' jaw tightened, and anger blew through him in a massive wave.

Kill, kill, kill, the amulet yelled in his mind.

With a yell so loud it might have been a roar, the bounty hunter sprinted toward Trevor. The other man tried to throw a punch, but James grabbed his arm, then smashed his elbow straight into the man's throat. After a sickening crunch, the glow left Trevor's eyes, and his body fell to the ground.

Yes, the amulet hissed. James twitched at the pure joy being broadcast into his mind over the death. Killing some asshole always satisfied him on some level, but he didn't get off on it like Whispy Doom.

He shook his head and glared down at the body.

"When will you assholes learn to never, ever threaten someone I love?"

James turned to help finish off Doug. He blinked, and his mouth fell open.

Now that I didn't expect to see.

The other man sported a large hole in the middle of his chest and a stunned expression on his face. He mouthed something, but no sound came out due to his lack of lungs.

Doug fell backward, dead.

James blinked several more times and looked at Shay. She held a silver candle holder. A few seconds later it turned to ashes, and a stiff breeze blew them into the wind.

"What the fuck was that?" the bounty hunter asked.

"A little backup. I didn't have time to run back and grab the *Masamune* from the truck. Plus, you should have paid more attention when I grabbed shit at Warehouse Five instead of looking for old barbeque shit." Shay shrugged. "I don't sell everything I find. So sue me."

16

Maria secured her helmet and harness as the helicopter's blades sped up and the vehicle lifted off the ground.

She surveyed the men on the chopper. Everyone wore their black armor and had their helmets on, the red of their goggles eerie in the darkened cabin. Anti-magic deflectors hung around their necks.

The rush to get the team on the transport helicopters had meant some sacrifices. They'd not have immediate tactical drone support from off-scene personnel, and they'd had limited weapon choices, but she wasn't that worried about apprehending a driver and a few people from a single van.

Just because these guys used a sleep spell doesn't mean shit. If they were really that tough, they would have just smashed into the museum and grabbed the artifacts. They are probably just a bunch of hired guns who'll surrender the minute AET lands.

Crap. Unless they've already weaponized some of those arti-

facts. Doubt AET tactical armor can take a direct hit from a damned tornado.

Maria shook her head. She needed to be realistic. If the men were that powerful, they wouldn't have run away when they realized they were being tracked.

Yeah. We can do this.

The pilot's voice came through her helmet receiver. "ETA fifteen minutes, Lieutenant."

"Good," she responded. She tapped her wrist control to change to the primary AET broadcast frequency. "Fifteen minutes until we catch up with the van. We'll give them one chance to surrender, then we take their asses down. If we're lucky, these guys will be spooked that we tracked them down and just give up. We know these people have access to magic even independent of the artifacts they stole. Keep in mind at all times these are enhanced threats and do not take them lightly."

"Yes, ma'am," the men transmitted through their helmet radios in near unison.

Even as she offered the warning, she smiled. The longer they flew, the less worried she became about the scumbags in the van being any sort of serious threat.

Maria grinned. It was time to for AET to prove a point to Spencer Preston.

Kathy leaned against the door of Tyler's office with her arms crossed and her face filled with curiosity.

Tyler ignored her as he typed away on his computer, only occasionally stopping to click the mouse or tap something on the tablet that was on the opposite side of his keyboard. He hated working with time constraints.

Man, this is obnoxious. No wonder Brownstone's so pissy half the time.

The brunette chuckled. "What are you doing?"

"There is the web, the dark web, the darker web, and the people I deal with. We know who is doing what above us, and I'm checking into that shit." Tyler shrugged.

"To do what, exactly?" She snorted. "You planning on running into another warehouse with Brownstone with a gun? You're a smart guy normally, but that wasn't a smart play."

Tyler shook his head. "No. I'm an information broker, so I'm finding fucking information. Cops and Brownstone all think about this shit the wrong way, because they're cops and he's a bounty hunter."

Kathy uncrossed her arms, a smile growing on her face. "Oh? What's the right way? I might give you crap now and again, but I'll never claim you're not a master information broker."

"Real sustainable crime's always about one thing in the end. You know what that is?"

She shook her head.

Tyler rubbed his thumb and finger together. "Money. They stole all this shit because they want to sell it. There was some obvious crap they threw out already. Too quick, not careful enough. It smells like a distraction. I'm sure the cops ate that up." He clicked his mouse. "But I found buyers for some of the other artifacts, way more hidden. I even know where they're going to be."

The information broker leaned over and tapped a button on the tablet.

Kathy narrowed her eyes. "What did you just do?"

"Sent an address to a number that I know will get passed on to Maria ASAP. Makes more sense to show up at the transfer location and ambush the guys that way." Tyler shrugged. "At least I think it does. Maybe the cops disagree. They can decide what they want to do with the information themselves."

"Why are you even getting involved at this point?" Kathy pinched the bridge of her nose and shook her head. "You're not getting paid, so you're violating your own principles, and whoever did this is obviously pretty well-connected, so if they find out that you were helping the cops, they're going to be pissed. Doesn't that violate neutrality?"

Tyler snorted. "The neutrality of the Black Sun extends to my parking lot, not all of fucking LA. Plus, they violated my neutrality when they took my girlfriend."

Kathy smirked.

"What?"

She shook her head. "Nothing. Your time to spend, but I better get back to the bar."

Maria grinned as her men jumped out of the helicopters on both sides of the parked delivery van and two blue SUVs. Three men in uniforms looked back and forth, while four bulky men in suits frowned.

She might not work gangs or organized crime as her

primary beat, but she knew Russian Mafia when she saw them.

Thanks, Tyler. With your help, we caught not just our thieves but a few bonus scumbags.

The AET advanced as the helicopters lifted back into the sky.

Maria kept her rifle trained on one of the men in uniform. Instinct told her they would be the greater threat if the situation went south. The other AET officers all aimed their weapons.

She activated her helmet mic. "This is the LAPD AET. We have you surrounded. You are to immediately drop any weapons and surrender. You're under arrest for grand larceny, conspiracy, kidnapping, attempted murder, and conspiracy to commit murder. Any sudden movements will be considered hostile actions, and you will be fired upon."

The lieutenant switched back to radio transmit mode.

Don't make this a pointless fight. We caught you with your pants down. The only thing left is to go to jail, assholes.

The lieutenant's stomach knotted. Every instinct in her screamed at once. She glanced around and spotted a ladder leading up the side of a warehouse.

"McCallister," she transmitted over her AET frequency. "Pull back and set up on that roof."

"Yes, ma'am." The AET officer jogged toward the roof, his sniper rifle slung over his back.

One of the gangsters raised his hands.

The other men frowned at him.

"What the hell are you doing?" one of the men in uniform asked.

The gangster shook his head. "They've got us. No point in dying here. Can't spend money when you're dead."

The other man snorted and cut through the air with his hand. A high-pitched whine accompanied the movement.

Maria thought the gangster was nodding, but a second later, her eyes widened at the horror she saw through her tactical goggles. The mobster's head fell to the ground, and his headless body toppled.

His killer sneered. "You're Russian. You should understand the principle of forced fighting well enough. Fight the enemy or die for your cowardice."

The rest of the Russians nodded and pulled out guns.

"Open fire!" Maria shouted.

Blue stun bolts and bullets flew from both sides to converge on the six remaining criminals. The bullets bounced off an invisible shield and the stun bolts dissipated, their energy arcing over the dome-shaped shield.

"Cease fire, cease fire."

One of the uniformed men grinned her way and held up his hand to reveal a brightly glowing rune. The third uniformed man reached into his pocket and pulled out a pen. He shook it, and it expanded into a silver wand.

"Fall back," Maria commanded. She pulled a sonic grenade off her tactical belt. "Activate your sonic dampeners."

This worked on a level five. It's going to work on you assholes.

She threw the grenade. It went off right before hitting the shield, but the men inside didn't fall down. The uniformed men actually had the balls to laugh, but the gangsters swallowed, sweat pouring down their faces.

The wizard and Mr. Air Blade spread out.

"Stun rifles," Maria barked. "Take turns shooting at them. We need to know exactly when that shield's down."

An officer blasted the shield, the dissipating energy clearly outlining it. Another fired a few seconds later.

"Anyone with grenades, feel free to nail those assholes the minute that shield is down."

Energy spread over the shield.

Maria raised her rifle and aimed at the man with the rune on his hand. They needed to make sure the bad guys couldn't pop off shots and then retreat behind their barrier.

Yet another officer fired, but this time his bolt zoomed right past the men.

"Open fire!" Maria shouted.

She squeezed the trigger, and the rune bearer jerked back with a grunt. Another bullet pushed him back, but not down.

Crap. Just die already, asshole.

Mr. Air Blade whipped his arm back and forth, and harsh whines sounded. Two officers flew back, grunts audible over the radio, their deflectors darkening. The bullets and bolts flying toward the enhanced threat jerked to the side or up at the last moment, and the attacks disappeared with a flash before reaching the body of the wizard with the silver wand.

More defensive magic?

Whatever magic the thieves were using hadn't been extended to the gangsters. They managed to get off a few shots before being struck by a storm of bullets and stun bolts. The attacks sent their bodies jerking and spinning as if they were performing some sickening dance before dropping to the ground, dead.

Maria flipped her rifle to burst fire and aimed at the head of the rune bearer. He'd been responsible for the main shield, and he might be responsible for the secondary magic. A quick burst put bullets into his head, and he stumbled back grimacing, blood leaking from his wounds.

"Sonic out," warned an AET officer. His grenade didn't accomplish any more than Maria's.

"Flashbang out," yelled another.

Maria kept firing. Her tactical goggles filtered out most of the flash.

Another two officers fell to the ground, victims of Mr. Air Blade. At least the man couldn't pull off the attack continuously.

The wizard raised his silver wand and muttered something. One of the SUVs floated into the sky.

Maria groaned. "Oh, for fuck's sake."

17

Shay glanced over her shoulder as James finished dragging the bodies next to the car. They wanted to get them out of sight in case some random family minivan pulled by and there were kids inside. She held her phone to her ear, still waiting for the Professor to respond to her last inquiry.

Wonder when the cops will show up? I know they knew we were on the guy and everything, but figured they'd want to come and collect this shit as soon as possible given that this museum heist was the highest-profile crime in the last few weeks in the city.

Shay glanced down at the artifacts she'd pulled out and described them to the Professor. There were a good number of them in several different bags and suitcases, including various wooden carvings of different races and animals, both Oriceran and terrestrial.

Crystal, wooden, and metal figurines formed a distinct grouping, along with figurines made of materials she couldn't even begin to hope to identify. Some were obviously meant to resemble people, places, or things, but others were odd geometric shapes that didn't look like anything natural. At least nothing on Earth.

An urn filled with a glowing blood-red liquid had been packed in one box by itself. Despite the car chase and the crash, there was no evidence it'd leaked or spilled.

Shay picked up the urn and slowly turned it until it was on its side. The liquid sloshed but didn't spill out.

Huh. That's neat. I should get one for my mantle.

A small number of paintings, drawings, and etchings formed yet another group. Some of the paintings looked normal. Others presented a true three-dimensional projection if they were facing upwards. One kept changing appearance. One of the drawings of a Kilomea, a huge ogre-like Oriceran species, not only had eyes that followed Shay when she moved, but the head even turned.

I hope that's not real. Yeah, maybe that poor bastard is trapped in there.

Shay shook her head. One problem that came with working so much around magic was that it helped her appreciate that there truly *were* fates worse than death.

I don't want to be killed in my kitchen by someone who claims to be my friend like I would have been if I'd stayed a killer, but I also don't want to end up stuck in a painting.

The Professor cleared his throat, signaling he was back on the call. "I apologize for the delay, Miz Carson, but I was just double-checking on the last few objects you described to me."

"Any of this shit important?" Shay asked.

He chuckled. "Importance is a relative thing. I can't say with absolute certainty, but all the objects you have described to me thus far are mostly what you'd call collectibles."

"Collectibles?" The tomb raider frowned. "What, like the Oriceran equivalent of Franklin Mint Civil War chess sets or fiftieth-anniversary plates?"

The Professor chuckled. "Some are like that, and others are more like the Mona Lisa."

"I don't get it. These guys weren't common thugs. If it weren't for James and me taking them on, they might have gotten away. They used serious magic for collectibles? I was expecting doom wands or something."

"It's not that hard to understand. Think of it this way, Miz Carson. If a group of thieves broke into the Louvre and stole the Mona Lisa, it's not like whoever they sold the painting to would be doing public showings of it, but it'd still be worth a lot of money." A distinct gulping and swallowing sound followed. "I suspect these items were similar. Most of their importance lies in who created them and their age, not in any unusual or dangerous powers associated with them. They were to be sold and shown to close associates in secret galleries, I suspect."

Shay snorted. "These guys fought to the death to protect fancy art?"

"People have killed others for far less. They do that every day in LA."

"True enough."

She sighed. "What's the plan? Do you want us to try to bring them to you, or should we just wait for the cops to pick them up?"

"The authorities collecting them is fine. Just don't leave them unattended until they arrive. The whole point of this little escapade is to make sure these objects aren't lost to the black market."

Shay snickered. "Yeah, don't want our world's supply of weird Oriceran art getting taken."

The Professor offered a chuckle of his own. "I'm more concerned about you and James finding some of the more dangerous artifacts like the Bowl of the Wind. I'm even more concerned with the fact that the museum's official records weren't accurate in regards to even minor artifacts such as these collectibles." He clucked his tongue. "Arrogance, duplicity, or ignorance. Perhaps all three."

Shay frowned. "What are you getting at, Professor?"

"I'm saying we can't even be sure what they had because I don't believe *they* knew what they had. This whole situation is rapidly closing on somewhere between a clusterfuck and a fiasco."

"Everyone needs a good clusterfuck now and again." Shay grinned and glanced at James, who kept rearranging the bodies. She had no idea what he was going for. Perfect symmetry, maybe? "Just go grab one of the blankets from your suitcases and put it over them already," she yelled.

James grunted and shrugged.

"Problem?" the Professor asked.

"Nope, just James being James."

"Pull fucking Johnson into cover," Maria yelled. She tapped her wrist control. "This is Lieutenant Hall, AET. Requesting immediate armed tactical drone backup at our current location."

She gritted her teeth. They should have been going after these guys with anti-magic bullets, but the damned brass had been bitching about budgets, and now her team was required to fill out paperwork to request anti-magic bullets before an operation. As if they'd always know exactly when they were going after a dangerous magic user.

You fucking bureaucrats got my men hurt today. I hope you're happy.

Two of her men rushed to their downed teammate. Johnson lay several yards from the SUV that smashed into him, his head and leg bent at unnatural angles and a pool of blood forming beneath him. They pulled him behind the SUV. Several other officers rushed to take advantage of the cover.

The lieutenant gritted her teeth as she looked at the mostly clear anti-magic deflector around his neck. The artifacts were designed to absorb magic, not impacts from multi-ton vehicles.

Other AET officers crouched behind the vehicle near a wall and behind a huge garbage bin.

Their muzzles flashed like cameras as they fired, mixing with the blue stun bolts in an eerie display of dangerous beauty. The dead gangsters had the courtesy to not get back up, but the other three men refused to go down.

Mr. Air Blade had taken a couple of minor hits, even though most bullets changed direction right before hitting him or cleared him. The rune bearer had multiple bullet wounds. Only the wizard with the silver wand seemed unscratched, though heavy perspiration dotted his brow.

At least the fucker's getting tired. We need to end this.

Weber, at the wall, sprinted toward the SUV. An invisible air blade slammed into him, and he cartwheeled through the air before slamming on the ground, his deflector now an inky black.

Maria rushed toward the sergeant, throwing her last flashbang toward the suspects. She kept her attention on her man as the bright flash lit the area. She hoisted the moaning Weber over her shoulder and ran toward the SUV.

Fuck, fuck, fuck.

She was half-tempted to call the helicopters back for an extraction, but if they came in now, the enhanced threats would just blow them out of the sky.

Maria swapped in a new magazine and put more bullets into the rune wielder, who, despite having dozens of bullet wounds at this point, remained standing.

"McCallister," she called through the radio. "Target the rune guy. Everyone concentrate on him."

"Roger that."

The echoing report of the sniper's .50 cal going off was heard even over the other gunfire. The rune bearer stumbled back, a huge new hole in his head.

Something slammed into Maria's leg, and she stumbled to the ground as pain spiked through her. She kept her arms wrapped around Weber and crawled behind the SUV, where a couple of other officers pulled her clear of the firing line.

The lieutenant hissed and sat up. A tire from the other SUV lay a few yards away. Their armor was helping them against the wizard tossing crap at them, but not enough.

Wonder why the fucker doesn't lift the first SUV again?

Maria glanced at the debris littering the battlefield. The asshole had thrown a car at them and every random-ass thing he could, but he'd not thrown anything twice.

That a weakness of his magic? A long cool-down? Don't know, but I have to pray that's what's happening.

She crawled over to Weber, ignoring the throbbing pain in her leg, and pulled off his helmet. Even though the sergeant was unconscious and blood trailed down his face from a forehead wound, he was still breathing.

Someone had already removed Johnson's helmet. His eyes were wide open and staring at the sky, and it was obvious from his bent neck he hadn't made it.

"Son of a bitch!" Maria punched the ground several times, the quick movement summoning new waves of pain from her leg.

The lieutenant pulled out an autoinjector containing a pain suppressant from a belt pouch, slammed into her neck, and pressed the button. She didn't have time to be injured. She had enhanced threats to put down.

I'm sorry, Johnson. I won't let those fuckers get away, no matter what.

Maria hissed as the needle shot into her neck, the cold flow of the drug tickling. She tossed the injector to the ground and forced herself to her feet.

She reloaded her rifle and flipped it to automatic, then rushed to the edge of the SUV. Another loud shot from McAllister sent the rune bearer to his knees. She didn't understand how he was even moving with a hole in his head.

Mr. Air Blade returned fire, and the sniper rolled back behind the lip of the roof.

The lieutenant's eyes widened as she saw something tumble from the roof to the ground. She snatched up her helmet and slammed it back on.

"McAllister, you all right?"

"I'm fine, Lieutenant. The bastard cut my rifle clean in half, though."

The pain in her leg fell to a dull ache. She stepped over to the corner of the SUV to add more bullets to the rune bearer's collection. Fifteen more seconds of sustained fire sent the man sprawling to the ground. The bastard finally stopped moving.

Maria narrowed her eyes, her heart thundering in her chest.

The telekinetic wizard flourished his wand, and the garbage bin some of her men had been using for shelter floated into the air. He grimaced and furrowed his brow. The officers all ran to the other side.

Running out of juice, huh, asshole?

"Concentrate on the wizard," Maria barked. She aimed low to compensate for recoil and held down the trigger.

Bullet after bullet flew toward the man from several angles, each disappearing in an increasingly brighter flash. Blood sprayed from his back as several bullets pierced his defense and his chest. He collapsed to the ground, the garbage bin crashing down with a resounding *thud* at the same time.

The lieutenant kept her finger on the trigger even after no more bullets came out, her drug-fogged brain taking a few seconds to realize it was empty.

Mr. Air Blade glanced at his fallen partners, his face scrunching in hatred. He threw his arms to his sides and screamed. A cloud of dust swirled around him, spinning faster and faster.

Maria slapped her last magazine into her rifle, switched to burst, and opened fire. She emerged from her cover. An air blade smashed into the SUV. Metal showered over her, bouncing off her armor.

Every few seconds she fired a controlled burst at the man's head, but her bullets, like everyone else's, kept changing course at the last moment. She advanced on the man.

"Lieutenant, fall back," someone called to her.

You killed one of my men, fucker. You don't leave this place alive.

Mr. Air Blade turned toward her, his face a mask of hatred.

Her gazed dipped for a moment at what she thought was an odd movement. It was actually the opposite. The dust swirling around him covered him from toe to head and extended up another yard, but there was a narrow strip right near his feet where no dust flowed.

Maria dropped to her stomach as he clapped his hands together. The very top of her helmet sparked and shot off, and the blade sliced into a nearby wall. If she'd waited just a half-second more, she would have joined the ranks of the headless.

But the lieutenant hadn't ducked to dodge. She'd hit the ground to aim better. It was time to avenge Johnson.

Maria aimed at his feet and squeezed off a burst. The man howled as bullets ripped into his foot and ankle and he fell to the ground, his dust devil disappearing. She flipped her gun back to auto.

Bullet and stun bolts rained down on him. The police didn't stop firing until there wasn't much recognizable left.

The lieutenant stood and yanked off her scalped helmet. She tossed it to the ground and limped over to the downed criminals. Her gun might be out of ammo, but she would bash in their damned skulls if she needed to. She dropped her rifle to the ground as she arrived at their bodies.

Nope. They were done. They wouldn't kill anyone ever again, and she hoped they were going through in-processing in Hell right now.

Maria stood for a few minutes just staring down at the bodies when someone called to her from behind.

"Lieutenant."

She turned slowly. The painkiller had kept her in action, but it clouded her thoughts more than she would have liked.

"What is it?" Maria asked.

The rhythmic whir of helicopter blades filled the night sky, along with the quieter whine of drones.

Too fucking late.

The officer looked down. "Johnson's dead. Lots of people are fucked up. Shelly's messed up, but he'll make it. Weber's up, but dizzy; probably broke a few things. Matthews can't feel anything below his waist. Got ambulances en route."

Maria scrubbed a hand over her face. "When the paramedics get here, have them use the transport choppers if they need to."

She took several deep breaths. She'd do what she needed to do to get healing potions or magic for them, cost be damned, but that wouldn't do anything for Johnson or his family.

Her jaw tightened. She had one weapon left, and she intended to use it.

Congratulations, Brownstone, you're going to get revenge for the AET.

18

James frowned down at the blanket covering the bodies. He was wasting a perfectly good emergency blanket on some assholes who should have been left for crows and rats to eat.

You fuckers don't deserve shit, but it wouldn't be nice to poison innocent animals with your tainted-ass meat.

The amulet had dropped into near silence, but the joy it took in his anger and hatred came through even without any words.

You liked that, huh? Whatever. You'll get plenty of killing before the night's over.

His phone rang, and he put it to his ear without checking the caller ID.

"This is Brownstone," he rumbled.

"James, this is Heather."

He sighed and took a deep breath. He didn't want to take out his anger on her.

"You got something for me?"

"Yeah, another van. They're only about thirty minutes from you, in Beverly Hills."

James frowned. "AET is closer, aren't they? Maybe you should tell them."

Heather sighed. "I was monitoring their communications, and from what I can tell they just got their asses handed to them. At least one cop is dead. Several wounded. They're going to need some time to rally."

The bounty hunter growled. "Lieutenant Hall?"

"She's alive, just banged up."

The amulet roused from its slumber.

Kill the enemy. Destroy the enemy.

James took a deep breath. "Did the assholes get away?"

"Nope, all dead on the scene."

Lucky for them.

"Give me minute by minute tracking by text," the bounty hunter offered, his voice so low he was practically infrasonic. "We'll handle the Beverly Hills van."

"Will do." Heather ended the call.

James gestured toward the truck. "Time to hit another set of assholes. AET took a beating, so they need a few minutes to get back on their feet."

Shay frowned. "What about the artifacts? The cops are still ten minutes away."

"Then call them and tell them to hurry the fuck up. We've got to go nail the next van while we still know where the bastards are." The bounty hunter stomped toward his truck. "These assholes aren't just thieves. They're also cop killers now."

Shay blew out a breath and hurried after him.

James hopped in the truck and started the engine. He

waited as Shay walked toward the vehicle, frowning as she spoke to the police.

She opened the door. "Okay. Thanks." She hung up. "They've got drone coverage here at least, and they'll be here soon. We've been given the okay to go after the next van."

He pulled onto the road and picked up his phone to check Heather's latest location text. "Beverly Hills, huh?"

His phone rang before he could set it down.

James grunted. "Alison? What the fuck?" He glanced at Shay. "You didn't tell her about this shit, did you?"

Shay shook her head. "Nope."

He sighed and answered the phone. "Hey, kid."

"Hey, Dad," she responded. "I'm totally sorry. I know I'm an awful daughter because I forgot to call you and let you know I got back to school safely."

"No, no, it's my fault. I should have called to check." James winced, suddenly feeling like a bad dad.

"Hey, is Aunt Shay with you?"

"Yeah." He glanced at the tomb raider.

Shay eyed him with curiosity.

"Can you put the phone on speaker?" Alison asked. "I want to talk to both of you."

"Sure, kid." James set it in the middle of his console and turned on the speakerphone. "What's up?"

Alison took a deep breath. "So, you want to tell me what's going on?"

He let an awkward chuckle. "What makes you think something's going on?"

She can't tell I'm lying over the phone, right?

Unknown, the amulet whispered back.

James frowned. He hadn't meant to ask it.

"Because I was looking at the news online, and it's all like, 'The Scourge of Harriken teams up with the LAPD to take down dangerous magical museum thieves.'"

He groaned. "They have that kind of shit out already?"

Shay laughed.

Alison snorted. "Don't think *you're* off the hook, Aunt Shay."

The tomb raider blinked. "Huh? What did I do?"

"Dad, are you wearing your amulet?"

James grunted. "Yeah."

Alison sighed. "Look, I've got my pendant. Dad's got his amulet. What do you have, Mom?"

"First of all, I'm not your..." Shay sighed. "Okay, I do have a few artifacts that can help, but I don't need one normally. I'm careful. Your dad's all about busting in doors and being direct. Sure, I like to get up close and personal when I have a heated discussion with someone, but I'm still a lot more careful than him."

"Oh, yeah, so careful that right now you're running around with Dad going after a bunch of guys who stole magic artifacts from a museum. According to the news, some are basically WMDs."

Shay rubbed the back of her neck. "That's kind of misleading. It's more about, you know..." She sighed. "Whatever. You are one tricky teenaged girl, Alison."

"Love you, too," the girl chirped back.

James shook his head. They needed to get the conversation off the topic of chaos in Los Angeles.

"You got to school okay?" he asked. "No problems? No

top-hat-wearing ferrets trying to pick your pockets or anything?"

Alison laughed. "The kind of Oricerans who can afford fancy clothes don't need to pick people's pockets, and yeah, everything went fine. Sure, I mean, there were travel delays, but, you know, that's just travel."

James smirked. He didn't need magic to know when someone was holding something back from him. If he hadn't spent a summer training Alison he might have demanded to know what she was hiding, but he decided that he didn't need the stress at the moment. It'd probably just involve him having to go throw some flirty boy off a magic train.

Shay smiled. "You excited to be back?"

"It's weird," Alison replied. "I'm happy to see my friends and teachers again, but I got used to living with you in LA and hanging out with the guys and everything." She laughed. "It's really low-stress hanging out at Camp Brownstone because all those guys are even more afraid to make a move on me than anyone at the school."

James grinned, far too satisfied with himself.

Shay rolled her eyes. "It's a good thing you're back at school and free of the overprotective influence of one James Brownstone."

Alison laughed.

Maria stood near the back of an ambulance. Her leg ached, the painkiller already starting to wear off.

A paramedic looked up from the unconscious officer he

was treating. "Lieutenant, even though it doesn't look like you broke anything, you should really be taking it easy."

She shook her head and pointed to a stretcher with an occupied body bag. "I lost a man. I won't fucking take it easy until everyone involved with this little museum gang is brought in or taken out."

The paramedic sighed and nodded. "You look a little pale. You sure you don't need a painkiller?"

Maria snorted. "I need my mind clear right now." She pointed to the officer. "You worry about him." She made her way to another ambulance.

Weber lay in the back, his head wrapped in bandages.

"You still remember who the hell you are?" the lieutenant asked.

"Yeah. They've got to run some neurological tests to be sure, but I think I made it out okay. But, shit, *Johnson*. And, hell, Matthews. I overheard one of the paramedics mentioning potential permanent paralysis."

Maria took several deep breaths. Magic had returned to the world, but it remained the same shitty place. Shittier, even.

It didn't seem fair. The US should be filled with witches healing people in hospitals and dragons flying kids to school, but mostly what she saw were rich assholes getting richer and criminals using magic to become deadly threats.

Earth still lumbered along like magic was indistinguishable from technology.

We don't have a fucking clue. Twenty years, and we're still acting like nothing changed. But everything *changed.*

Weber sighed. "Look, Lieutenant, everyone who joins AET knows the score. It's not like it's easy, but at least we took those guys down with us. Imagine if some patrol cops had run into them. They would have been dead in seconds."

"Yeah." Maria nodded. "I'm sure that'll help Johnson's family feel better. I don't care who I have to throw at them now, though. All these assholes are going down."

Weber chuckled and then winced. "Guess it's too early for me to be laughing, but you're really talking about throwing Brownstone at them?"

"Yeah. I also just heard a few minutes ago that the small team I sent to support the Major Crimes and Vice raid did okay. No injuries. We got all those artifacts, but I think we've lost the element of surprise. Brownstone and Shay wasted the two guys they ran into. I was worried I might have to justify him killing them with paperwork since they aren't bounties yet, but after all this shit, I don't think anyone's going to care if these museum guys end up dead." She nodded. "These guys are a clear and present danger to the public, and I won't let them get away, no matter what I have to do. So, yeah, time for Brownstone to do what he does best."

Logan wanted to smash his phone against the ground. How the fuck had this all happened? They'd planned this operation well, but everything was going completely to shit.

He took a few deep breaths. Failure was part of all high-risk operations. He understood that. Tak had to understand that, too.

Logan gritted his teeth. Lying to others was one thing,

but lying to yourself was pathetic. Every man on his team understood that it was better to die than surrender to the police. Tak and his shadow bosses would make sure that anyone who surrendered on a job would suffer a painful death no matter where they tried to hide.

He should know. He'd already seen it.

The man sucked in a breath. They could salvage the situation. The only significant loss thus far was the circlet. Some minor losses in funds could be made up for by pay cuts. The artifacts of true importance hadn't been recovered.

Logan lifted his phone and took a deep breath. At least he'd survive to the end of the job. It wasn't like Tak could handle the men directly. If he could, Logan wouldn't be there.

He dialed Tak and waited.

The dwarf answered on the first ring. "Explain to me why I'm hearing things I really wish I wasn't. It's almost like the universe is conspiring to give me a bad day."

Logan cleared his throat. "I'll admit there have been some complications."

"Elaborate."

"The police and Brownstone have raided several of the vans and transfer points." Logan took a deep breath. "As far as the vans go, everything but the research and vault artifacts has been secured by the authorities or Brownstone. All our men have been killed except for the team in the decoy van. They abandoned the van and the police have discovered it, leaving them with two empty vans. I'm having the vault artifact van pick those men up for reinforcements."

Tak sighed. "So what you're telling me is that much of the financial benefit of the job has already evaporated, which will impact future operations. Many of the men working this job are also highly trained and hard to replace. Does all that sound correct to you, Logan?"

"Yeah, it does." He rubbed the back of his neck, happy the dwarf hadn't insisted on a video call.

"And what of the specialty artifacts?"

"Those are safe." Logan let out a sigh of relief. At least he had some good news to report. "We got those transferred to the SUV, and there's nothing to indicate the cops know about them."

Tak chuckled. "Was there anything that indicated the police knew about the vans?"

"Well, no, but—"

"You will fix this," the dwarf hissed. "If you can't fix it, end my trouble for me. Do you understand?"

The man gritted his teeth. "Yeah. I understand."

Tak ended the call.

Logan stared at the phone. Ending Tak's trouble would mean Logan eating the end of his gun. If he didn't, the dwarf would make sure he suffered before he died.

Logan shook his head. He grabbed his phone and texted the drivers of the two remaining vans and the SUV.

Grab additional weapons and artifacts and go to Plan C. Use the illusion powder and the resonant teleport beads. I'll take responsibility for the cost

The drivers of one of the vans and the SUV texted back a simple **OK**

The other van didn't respond for several seconds. Logan frowned when he read the text.

Brownstone is already on our tail. Don't have time to pull over and use the items

Logan texted back, **I've got an idea. Make sure you do exactly what I say**

19

James grunted as they closed on their next target. The van had sped up but wasn't trying to swerve or take any other obvious evasive action. He wasn't sure what to make of that.

Like you assholes are gonna outrun my F-350 in a delivery van anyway. Just give the fuck up.

The bounty hunter snorted and pushed down the gas pedal. The whole situation was ridiculous as they sped along surface streets past gated communities and multi-million dollar homes. Maybe the thieves had hoped that staying in a ritzy residential zone would lower the chance of anyone noticing them and calling the police.

Surprised I don't have some asshole calling to beg me not to show up in their neighborhood like that fucker did when the hitmen were after me.

Shay pointed to the van. "Just ram him already."

James shook his head. "Don't want to ram too many of these fuckers. Might mess up my truck."

Shay rolled her eyes. "Yes, I'm sure it'd be awful if you have to get a truck that was made this decade."

The van screeched around the corner. James yanked on his wheel to follow.

His phone rang, and he nodded at it. "Answer that. Don't want to take my hands off the wheel while we're chasing them."

Shay picked up the phone. "Huh. It's from Maria." She touched the screen to answer it. "We're right behind the next van. Yeah. Yeah." She nodded. "I understand. I'll pass it along. Thanks, you too."

She ended the call and set the phone down with a smirk.

James glanced her way after another hard turn to keep up with the van. "What'd she say?"

"We should execute the capture with extreme prejudice. She wants those fuckers to go down, and that 'Brownstone should do what I think he does so well.'" Shay's smirk disappeared. "There are times when the only way to fight a monster is with another monster. We've got a responsibility to become those monsters and do bad things to bad people now."

The bounty hunter grunted. "I've got no problem taking down assholes. It was my plan anyway. Glad everyone else is on board with it."

Kill, the amulet chanted.

Yeah, working on that. Keep your tendrils on.

James tried to focus on the road. At least the amulet shut up when he actually started killing people. It was almost like it was too busy soaking in happiness to talk. It claimed it'd somehow strengthened his skin at the expense of his telekinesis. Maybe the last fight would have been harder without the modifications.

This shit's getting more complicated. Guess there's no simple way to have a living amulet that modifies your body.

He snorted and shook his head before taking a corner to keep up with the van.

"What?" Shay asked.

"Nothing. Just thinking."

Shay nodded, undid her tactical harness, and stripped off her shirt. She tossed the burned and hole-filled mess into the back before pulling another shirt out of a suitcase, along with her adamantine knives. She slipped the knives into three sheaths on her harness and put on the shirt.

James smiled a little. Too bad she wasn't going to get completely naked, but that might have been too much to ask for since they were hurtling along surface streets at sixty miles per hour chasing artifact thieves.

The tomb raider winked at him. "Get through this, and you'll find out what it feels like when your mind goes to the moon while your body is in bed."

He chuckled. "Better stay alive then."

The van blew through a red light, as did James, but fortunately there was no cross-traffic. A little collateral property damage was one thing. Innocent people getting hurt wasn't acceptable.

"Wonder when these fuckers are gonna give up?" the bounty hunter rumbled. "We're pulling out of the neighborhood. Maybe he's gonna hit the highway. They haven't even shot at us."

Shay waved a hand. "Just ram him already. You can buff out the dents."

James grunted. "Easy for you to say. You don't love your car like I love this truck."

"First, a man should not love his truck. And, yeah, I don't love my car that much because I have like fifty of them. They are just a fancy way to get from Point A to Point B." Shay sighed and frowned pensively.

Shit. This seems like a podcast moment. Uh, what should I do? Oh, yeah. "Asking questions is never wrong. Trying to force a solution is. She'll want to know that you care about her emotions and thoughts."

"You okay?" James asked.

The van accelerated, and he matched their speed.

Shay nodded as she checked her 9mm. "Yeah. Just funny how since I stopped being a professional killer, I kill more people than ever. If not working with you, then on tomb raids. I've been trying to dial some of this down, especially when Lily's with me, but it's not like everyone or everything I run into on my jobs can be convinced to not try to kill me."

James shrugged. "Like you said, sometimes monsters need to take out other monsters. You that worried about it?"

"Nah. Not really." The tomb raider smiled and holstered her pistol. "My past doesn't define me anymore. It's what taught me the skills I use to defend myself, my friends, and my family. I'm Shay Carson, just with a badass wicked alter ego."

James shrugged. "Don't care. Love you in all ways, and you'll have to kill a lot more people if you want to reach my count."

Shay snorted. "Keep in mind I was with you for the final Harriken assault, not to mention the cartel."

He grinned. "Just saying."

The tomb raider reached over to pat him on the shoulder. "That's one thing that has helped me learn to be me. There's nothing I could do that would shock you."

James shook his head. "I might be scared if you do that thing in the sex book you showed me."

Shay burst out laughing. "Oh, you can't handle the power of the *101 Nights of Kinky Sex*?"

He grinned.

Still snickering, she pointed to the van. "Looks like our boys are turning into that parking garage. It's gonna be hard for them to lose us in there."

James chuckled. "Good, they finally want to stop being pussies. Glad to take them up on that. At least this way I don't have to dent my truck."

Shay laughed. "Maybe I should be giving you the book *101 Nights of Kinky Truck Sex*."

Peyton's fingers flew over his keyboard. He wasn't used to not having a direct comm line to Shay, but she'd told him to concentrate on finding the last van and to leave everything else to James and her.

Maybe it was habit or a desire to feel out the competition, he'd instead contacted Heather to chat with her while they both worked the job.

We can do this. Two hackers are better than one, right?

Peyton blew out a breath. "I've got bots searching through camera and drone footage for Andercarr delivery vans with suspicious plates through the west half of the county now. You've got everything covered in the east, right?"

"Yes," Heather replied. "Getting a lot of hits on vans, but all with normal plates."

"Huh. Maybe they figured out we were homing in on them because of the plates."

Heather sighed. "I doubt it. Every plate I run through the system is registered with Andercarr. If they'd stolen actual company vans, they wouldn't have had to disguise them in that warehouse, right?"

"Yeah. Good point." Peyton picked up a piece of the freshly made pepperoni pizza and took a bite. There were many fringe benefits to being the Pizza King, but having great food was the major one. He swallowed. "I've been trying to track weird reports as well."

"Weird reports?"

He took another bite before responding. "Yeah. When magic's involved, sometimes you get weird stuff. I was hoping they were using artifacts and leaving a trail of wackiness. Shay and I have seen that kind of thing before."

Heather laughed. "It's a good idea, but we're in LA. It's Freaktown, USA. How are you going to notice something weird against all the background weirdness?"

"It's an idea in progress. You trying anything else?"

"Working on trying to hack into satellite image data. I was hoping that if I can get the data and then filter for the vans, that I could just kind of follow their path. It's going to take me a while, though."

Peyton set his pizza down. "Not any longer than

filtering through all the background weirdness. Too bad there are no general magic detection satellites or drones."

He smirked. They didn't exist *yet*, but given what he knew about Project Nephilim and Project Ragnarok, he wouldn't put it past the government to develop something like that sooner rather than later. For all he knew, Amber was helping some project create one.

Heather sighed. "We could use drones to do different types of scans. Do these artifacts give off any unusual heat or EM radiation?"

"Not that I know of, and it's still going to be too hard to filter through the all background crap in LA." He frowned. "At least without having some general idea where the last van might be. I guess I'll keep at monitoring weirdness reports and looking for Andercarr vans. Also going to send a few bots into the dark web to poke around see if there's any talk of other transfers or sales. Kind of doubt it after the cops hitting that first one so quickly, but it won't hurt to try."

Heather chuckled. "You sound like we're losing. Look, between the cops, James, and Shay, they've found four out of five vans."

"Yeah, but a couple of those were empty."

"They were probably just the vans that had already delivered the artifacts. The cops grabbed a bunch at the first raid." Heather tapped at her keyboard a moment, the clack coming loudly over the line. "And two other vans *were* filled with artifacts. Good bet the last one is too, so we just need to stop whining and find it. I came home early from my vacation for this crap."

Peyton sighed. "You're right. Let's do this thing."

The van screeched to a halt in the darkened and shadow-filled parking garage. James stopped the F-350 a good hundred feet away and pulled to the side. The last couple of guys had been tougher than he'd anticipated. He wasn't worried for himself, but his poor truck couldn't defend itself, and it'd already been through a lot in the last year.

Rows of vehicles filled the parking lot. At least they'd have a lot of cover.

Guess I'm gonna have to pay out a lot of my money from the job to people for their cars getting damaged.

Kill the enemy, Whispy Doom chanted.

Don't need to be told that. Just wait a fucking second.

James threw open his door and jumped out. Shay followed, this time kitted out with both her adamantine knives and her enchanted *tachi*. She reached into a box in the back and pulled out a few other small items, including a gold ring inscribed with glyphs.

"I underestimated the last guys," Shay commented as she slipped the ring on and closed the door "This ring might not be as useful as Whispy Doom, but it should at least help me." She sighed. "And ignore the next part. It doesn't mean I'll be going to church with you."

"Huh?"

"You'll see." Shay held up her right palm. "Michael to my south. Gabriel to my west. Uriel to my north. Raphael to my east. Grant me thy protection." The ring glowed brightly for several seconds, then a pulsing gold aura surrounded Shay.

James smirked. "Yeah. I'll have you confessing to Father McCartney soon."

"I'd burst into flames if I stepped into a church." Shay frowned. "It's just the incantation. I didn't make the thing."

James grunted. "Now we can both go all-out."

"Yeah, by the time this job is over, I'll be lucky to break even. Even limited-use objects are expensive as shit, you know."

The bounty hunter shrugged. "You should look into getting yourself a whispering amulet of doom."

"Very funny."

Shay narrowed her eyes as five men filed out of the van. Two held guns, and the other three held wands. Footsteps echoed as a dozen more men carrying a variety of weapons marched around the corner. Most held pistols or rifles, but a few were carrying RPGs or rocket launchers.

James grunted. He yanked out his .45, sprinted away from his truck, and ducked behind a Dodge pickup on the other side of the row. "Guess we know now why they didn't try that hard to lose us."

"Sonofabitch," the tomb raider muttered. She frowned at James. "Why did you run over there?"

"Don't want them to use that rocket launcher on my truck." James shrugged.

Shay rolled her eyes and found cover behind a red Porsche, yanking out her pistol.

That's love, when your woman tries to avoid getting your truck blown up.

"I figure we take out the small fry first, then focus on the magic users," Shay suggested.

"Whatever ends with them all down is fine by me."

One of the wizards stepped forward and raised his wand, a smirk on his scarred face. "Looks like you're a little outnumbered, Brownstone."

The bounty hunter snorted. "I was outnumbered when I took on the Harriken, too."

The wizard snorted. "A bunch of pathetic gangsters." He nodded at the other two men with wands. "Three wizards, Brownstone, and two gun mages. Not to mention all our friends here."

James shrugged. "Lars Hansen had a bunch of souped-up guys with him, too. You should go find a necromancer so you can ask him how well that worked out for him."

The scarred wizard narrowed his eyes. "Got any last words, Scourge of Harriken?"

New damage, the amulet whispered. *Adapt and become stronger.*

"Yeah, I do." James shook his head. "You know what I'm fucking sick of? All you assholes think that you've got something new to bring me. You think you're gonna take me out, but then you just end up dying. If you're gonna talk a big game, you should actually bring it, fuckers."

The wizard shouted an incantation, and a bolt of lightning blasted from the wand and struck James' shoulder. He flew back and slammed into the car behind him, the window cracking.

Fuck. Glad they didn't have a car alarm.

The bounty hunter stood and winced. Whispy Doom was doing something approaching laughing in his mind. He understood why. The amulet had been well-trained on electricity, thanks to Shay.

One of the other wizards, a skinny guy with a porn-star

mustache, launched a white-hot orb of flame at the bounty hunter. James didn't even bother to dodge.

He winced as the orb slammed into him, stinging him with a light burn. He'd soloed King Pyro while wearing his amulet. These guys would have to do a lot better with fire and heat to hurt him.

The third wizard frowned but didn't attack.

The non-wizards stared at James, their mouths open. They'd obviously expected him to be dead already.

"That all you got?" James snorted, whipped up his gun, and opened fire. Shay joined him.

The enemy's rifles and pistols came alive, and bullets sparked near both groups. Windows shattered. Three of the thugs went down within seconds, rounds to their heads or chests. Only one man with a heavy weapon, Mr. RPG, was left.

Several bullets zipped right past James, only to turn around and strike him in the back. They stung but didn't accomplish much. A pile of half-melted bullets lay beside Shay as well. Her angel ring was keeping her safe.

James almost wanted to laugh. The two gun mages looked confused and frustrated.

"Got to do better than just shoot me in the back," the bounty hunter taunted.

James rushed away from the Dodge as Mr. RPG lined up his weapon. The shot hissed through the air and blew the Dodge onto the vehicle next to it, forming a fiery pyre of melted metal.

The car beneath survived, but its blaring alarm joined the cacophony of the battle. The alarm died a moment later when the scarred wizard delivered a zap.

"Close your eyes, James," Shay shouted.

Do not close, the amulet ordered. *Adjusting.*

Listening to strange alien amulets was probably a bad idea, but James did it anyway. He winced as pain shot through his eyes.

Shay ducked into the next row of cars and threw a flashbang. One of the other wizards mumbled an incantation, and the grenade bounced back before going off.

The following bright flash blinded their opponents, but James' vision cleared up in less than a second.

Fuck. That's cool.

Reverting vision defense, the amulet whispered.

James hissed as pain struck his eyes again. He shook his head.

Why not just leave it on?

Insufficient resources.

The criminals were less prepared than the bounty hunter. The entire group of men stumbled back. One man accidentally shot another in the face.

Shay laughed. "Different ways to take guys down. Damn. I wish I had another on me. I have more in my box." She gunned down one of the men.

James shook his head. "Don't you dare go near my truck until they're all dead."

"Whatever." The tomb raider squeezed off a few more rounds, and two more men collapsed to the ground. She tried to nail one of the wizards and the bullet bounced off an invisible shield, but her two quick center-of-mass shots at the gun mages had them flat on their backs in a pool of their own blood a moment later.

Idiots. Should have worn a bulletproof vest.

The amulet continued to burble happily but quietly in the back of James' mind, pleased with the death-dealing in the parking lot.

The bounty hunter didn't bother with any of the wizards. He methodically aimed and fired at their backup, sending four men to the ground, blood spraying from head wounds.

The third wizard made careful and quick moves with his wand, and a blue haze surrounded the men. Their instant change in stance and improved aim ended Shay's and James' shooting gallery fun.

Oh, he's just there to keep them alive, huh?

James and Shay both nailed the sucker with a rifle at the same time, the bounty hunter in the chest, the tomb raider in the head. He spun like a top before falling.

No shield. Too bad.

The rifleman joined the other eleven bodies on the ground. By now, their blood had pooled together to form a crimson lake.

Every car in the area was riddled with bullets and had new red paint jobs. The delivery van's windows were shattered, and its back wheels were both flat. Several cars were on fire.

A bolt of lightning missed Shay by inches. She ducked, reloaded, and shoved her gun in her holster.

"Down to three versus two," James shouted. "It was unfair before for you, and now it's even more fucking unfair."

The wizards all raised their wands and chanted something in Latin in unison.

"Whatever, you can keep trying to use a lightning bolt. That shit's not gonna work on me."

The chanting increased in speed and volume. James tried to put the wizards down, but his bullets just kept bouncing off.

The bounty hunter holstered his pistol. "Fuck. I think we're gonna have to get close. Even if I can't get through with my fists, I can distract them, and you can use the sword."

"Try this."

She pulled out an adamantine knife and tossed to him. James snatched it out of the air. He liked the weight and balance.

Shay's hand dropped to the hilt of her sword.

The wizards finished their chant. A glowing translucent image of a massive dragon's head appeared in front of them.

"What the fuck is that?" James muttered.

"Something not fun," Shay suggested.

Joy blasted from the amulet. *Adaptation.*

The dragon spat a pulsating blue-green orb. The bounty hunter leapt back, as did Shay. The orb smashed into his previous location, exploding in a massive wave of blue fire. The wave slammed into James and sent him flying into the air.

He grunted in pain as he crashed to the ground between the rows of cars and directly in the path of the enemies. The front of his shirt had been incinerated, and the smell of his burned flesh filled his nostrils. Cuts covered his body.

Not just normal fire, huh? Shit. Glad I have a spare shirt in the truck.

Yes, the amulet hissed. *New damage. Grow stronger.*

Whispy Doom's exhilaration continued to flood into James.

I feel like I just went through a shower of burning knives, and you're happy?

Adaptation. Grow stronger.

Shay lay several yards away, not in as bad of shape, but still bleeding from several wounds. Her glow had vanished, and her ring had turned to wood.

Guess she's out of power.

The dragon's head vanished, and the scarred wizard laughed.

"You had me worried there for a minute, Brownstone. I actually thought we might not be able to beat you." He tapped his wand in his palm. "You know what, though. The best part about this is that this isn't over. After all, you think I don't watch the news? Think I didn't hear all about that little half-Oriceran bitch you adopted?"

James gritted his teeth and let out a low growl.

Kill the enemy, the amulet roared in his mind. *Destroy the enemy.*

The wizard raised his wand and took a few steps forward. He waved some smoke from the nearby burning car out of his face. "You don't realize who you are fucking with this time, Brownstone. We're going to kill you here, then we're going to track down your little daughter. We'll kill her nice and slow, and the entire time we're going to tell her it's Daddy's fault."

James pushed himself off the ground, only distantly

aware of the pain beneath the storm of rage in his mind. Shay shouted something, but he didn't even register it. There was only one thing that he cared about at that moment—killing the motherfucker who had just threatened Alison.

Yes, yes, yes, the amulet hissed. *Sufficient power.*

20

Shay blinked as she watched James.

Shit, the tomb raider thought. *I always knew there was more to that thing.*

Silver-green tendrils shot from the amulet embedded in his chest. The tendrils flattened and spread out, covering his chest, back, and right arm with a textured metallic silver-green second skin. A glowing spike covered his right hand and forearm.

Shay tried to push her pain out of her mind and pull her sword. She needed to help James before he got himself killed. Just because Whispy Doom had new tricks didn't mean the bounty hunter couldn't be killed.

The scarred wizard stepped back with a frown. "Guess you still have a few cards to play, Brownstone? Doesn't matter. You're wounded, and you're still going to die. I like seeing you struggle. It's more fun this way. I'm sure it'll be like that with the girl, too."

A bolt of lightning followed. It struck James square in the chest. He stumbled back but didn't flinch. Another bolt followed. Then another. The electricity crackled around the bounty hunter.

He only growled in response.

Porn-star Wizard tried a few fireballs to help his friend. They slammed into James' chest, darkening the armor there, but not doing much more. Another shot nailed his uncovered upper thigh, burning through his jeans and singing the skin underneath.

James stalked forward, raising his right arm and the spike.

The support wizard swallowed and raised his wand to summon a glowing red shield between James and the men. It cut across the entire parking garage, including through several vehicles, but it didn't damage them.

The bounty hunter tilted his head and stared at the scarred wizard, not saying anything.

Shay pulled out her *tachi.* "Take cover before they use the other spell again."

James didn't even look at her. He let out a low growl and charged the wizards.

You idiot. They just put up a barrier.

Fire and lightning struck him every few seconds as the panting wizards finished their incantations, but he continued closing. He slammed right into the red barrier and bounced back.

The magical attacks stopped, and the scarred wizard laughed again. He wiped the sweat off his forehead. His quick casting was obviously taxing him.

The man sneered. "Desperation isn't a strategy, Brownstone."

Shay ducked and crept toward the men in the small

amount of space behind the cars. She hoped the field was weaker at the edges.

James stood and slammed his spike into the field. It pierced the barrier with a flash.

The tomb raider blinked and stopped moving forward.

What the hell?

James slashed back and forth until the barrier vanished.

The support wizard's eyes widened. "Impossible."

The bounty hunter sprinted toward the man and impaled him through the head. He yanked the spike out and spun toward the other men. They stumbled backward, both throwing another attack at his leg. The blackened flesh of his thigh suggested a serious injury, but he continued stalking forward, his eyes locked on the men.

With a blur, the spike became a flat silver-green blade. After a quick slice, Porn-star Wizard's head fell from his body.

The scarred wizard kept walking backward as James advanced on him. A cement pillar stopped his escape.

"What the fuck are you, Brownstone?" the man yelled.

James roared and sliced the man's head off, but his attack didn't end. He kept hacking and slashing the man's body. The man's blood splattered all over him as he continued.

Shay sheathed her blade and jogged over to the bounty hunter. "It's over, James. They're all dead."

He spun, growling slightly. "Alison."

The tomb raider held up her hands. "Is safe at the school. She's safe, and these guys are all dead. It's all over."

"Alison," James repeated. He let out another low growl and glared at the pieces of his last victim.

Shay sighed. "She's safe."

The bounty hunter gave her a faint nod. The new armor and weapon retracted, and he took several deep breaths.

"You okay?" Shay asked.

James nodded. "Yeah. Just got a little pissed, is all."

"Yeah, I'll say." She shook her head.

It's like Whispy Doom got stronger because of his anger. Do we really want him using a weapon that requires him to fucking lose his shit?

Heather frowned as she stared at the various bright circles on her screen. "Peyton, I think I've got something."

He mumbled, but she couldn't understand him.

She rolled her eyes. "Even my son knows to not talk with his mouth full."

"Sorry," Peyton replied. "What do you mean, you think you've got something?"

"I was filtering through some satellite data, and I've got a general direction the last van was going. From what I can tell, it headed to Mar Vista."

A crunching sound came over the line.

"What now?" Heather asked.

"Wanted some chips, too. Textural counterpoint, you know? Mar Vista, huh? One second."

This time she only heard typing and not crunching.

Peyton laughed. "And you mocked the weirdness reports."

Heather blinked. "You're serious? It worked?"

"Kind of."

"Define 'kind of.'"

Peyton chuckled. "Some old woman with too much time on her hands complained to a local neighborhood board about suspicious delivery vans in the area. She says she's seen one circling the area, and she thinks it's part of a human trafficking plot."

Heather frowned. She immediately clicked to another window on her second monitor to find cameras and drone feeds in Mar Vista. "She didn't call the cops?"

"No. She doesn't trust the cops, because she says, and I quote, 'The cops are all controlled by the Illuminati, who are controlled by gnomes from Zurich who came over from Oriceran a thousand years ago.'"

"Sounds like a real credible witness." Heather snickered. "But, for all we know, she's right."

"Maybe she's right about gnomes, but she says it was an Andercarr van. Apparently, UPS isn't controlled by the Illuminati, but Andercarr is. She got a license plate number." He rattled it off.

Heather clicked to the Andercarr database she'd hacked and entered the number. "Guess what?"

"What?"

"That van isn't owned by Andercarr."

Peyton laughed. "Score one for crazy old ladies."

Heather smirked and found several drone feeds. She started feeding their footage into her search algorithm. "Race you to finding the van."

"You're on."

The hacker continued sending data to her algorithm as she moved from camera to camera and drone to drone. The bastards were there. They just had to find them.

"Got it," they yelled in unison ten seconds later.

Heather frowned as she looked at the screen. "Shit."

Peyton chuckled. "You go ahead and make the call. You need to develop your 'giving Brownstone good news and bad news' skills."

"Okay." Heather pulled her headset off and grabbed her phone. She dialed James.

"Yeah?" James rumbled on the other end.

He sounds pissed. Then again, he always sounds kind of pissed.

Heather rubbed the back of her neck. "Good news is, Peyton and I found the last van."

"What's the bad news?"

"It's already backed up to a warehouse."

James snorted. "Nah. That's great fucking news."

"It is?"

"Yeah. It means we don't have to chase their asses."

Dannec's eyes darted back and forth as he handed Maria the potion. They still stood in the aftermath of the last attack, uniformed officers and police cars all over the area. CSI had also arrived, but the contract forensics mage they had on staff was nowhere in sight.

"That's it? One potion?" Maria frowned.

The elf shrugged. "I'm not a magical pharmacy, Lieutenant, and just so you know, that's a minor potion. It'll help you if you're a little banged up, but it's not going to help your seriously wounded men at the hospital."

"Well, fuck. Thanks for nothing."

The elf shook his head and tapped the deflector hanging on her chest. "Just keep in mind that without my help, a lot more cops would have died tonight."

Maria gave him a nod. "Yeah, you're right." She eyed the potion and then downed it.

Dannec raised an eyebrow.

"If it can't really help my men, then I need to heal myself, because I need to be there when we take down the last of these bastards." The pain in her leg started to ebb. "Brownstone and Shay took out a whole batch of them, and they found a shitload of artifacts."

The elf frowned. "AET took a heavy beating today. How are you going to go after anyone else?"

"I sent a small team to a different site. They aren't hurt, and we've got enough people from this team who are more than willing to volunteer even if they are a little scratched up." Maria shrugged. "And if we know where the bastards will be, we can have better equipment ready, too."

The elf reached into his pocket and pulled out a small handkerchief. The cloth expanded into a laden bag. He handed it to Maria.

She took the bag and opened it. It was filled with rifle magazines. "What the hell is this?"

"We had a discussion not all that long ago where you mentioned a shortage of anti-magic bullets. You'll be paying for these, of course, but I thought it might help." Dannec gave her a polite nod. "Now I have to leave. I'm allergic to all this law enforcement."

The elf turned and started walking toward the street.

She watched him go until an indicator on her wrist control informed her that her phone was ringing. Without her helmet, she'd have to take the call the old-fashioned way. She pulled her phone out of her tactical belt and looked at the caller ID.

"Hey, Shay," she answered. "Something else turn up?"

"We just got word from some of our info people. They've got the location of the last van."

Maria's heart rate kicked up. "We can block those roads off, and I can have another team ready to go within minutes."

"They're not moving. They're at a warehouse in Mar Vista."

The lieutenant grinned. "Even better. Look, I need to know if Brownstone is joining the party."

"Yeah. He's definitely in an ass-kicking mood."

"Good." Maria shook the bag full of anti-magic bullet magazines. "Just got a refill that might help. I just have to make one more call and get a new helmet."

"Sounds like a party. Let's finish this shit."

Maria chuckled. "Agreed. See you soon."

She hung up the phone and took a deep breath. It was time to skip past the bureaucrats and go directly to the Chief. A cop was dead, and many others hurt.

You're going to give me what I need.

2 1

S hay gestured to the back of the van as a police officer continued to take notes on his tablet. "Sorry about the bullet holes in the van, and we'll pay for any of the damaged cars. Those guys really didn't want to surrender."

The officer shrugged. "They already killed one cop tonight. I'm not gonna cry over them." He peered at the boxes, suitcases, and bags filled with artifacts in the back. "Man, all that shit's magical, huh? Some of it looks weird but not all that magical."

The tomb raider nodded. "Yeah. It's magical enough to steal and kill for."

He shook his head. "Some days, I wish I could be a cop, you know, just back in like 2018 or some shit. Before all this magic, you know? Safer time. Simpler time."

Shay chuckled. "Safer maybe, probably not simpler, from what I've read." She shrugged. "Then again I don't know. I was a little girl."

"I was a teenager." The cop took a deep breath and looked over his shoulder at James, who was leaning against a pillar, his arms crossed, He was still covered in blood, but he'd put on a new shirt before the police arrived. His gaze kept darting from James to the remains of the scarred wizard. Even though several heavily damaged bodies lay around, bullet-riddled or sliced up, the dismembered corpse was easily the goriest sight in the parking garage.

"Got something you want to ask?" Shay sighed. "Just spit it out."

The cop blew out a breath. "Look, just, you know that shit over there? It's pretty intense. What the fuck happened? It looks like Brownstone tore the guy apart."

"It'd be more accurate to say he sliced the guy apart, but yeah. That's what happened."

"Why? That's something an animal would do, and you got other guys missing heads." The cop shrugged.

Shay frowned. "We were just taking them on, and they got cocky and threatened to torture and kill his daughter."

The cop's face hardened. He turned toward the body, crossed himself, and spat on the ground. "Fuck the guy, and fuck the rest of these rats. I've got a daughter, so I know what he must have felt like. They can all rot in hell as far as I'm concerned."

Her phone chimed with a text. "Sorry, I'm expecting something from Lieutenant Hall."

The man nodded. "I've got to talk to some of the other officers anyway. We'll contact you if we need any more information."

"Thanks."

Shay looked at the text.

Arming up now, have a team assembled. Smaller

than normal. Need to know 100% if you're still in. Need to coordinate our chopper arrival with your arrival

The tomb raider glanced at the frowning James before tapping back her response.

We're in. We'll head out in a couple of minutes and I'll text you with our ETA

Okay. See you soon

Shay slipped the phone back into her pocket and walked over to James. "Hall just texted me. She's raring to go. Because of that beating, though, the AET isn't at full strength. You still in for another round?"

"Yeah," James rumbled. "A round or two. I'm not stopping until all these fuckers are caught or dead."

"Even if you go all…" The tomb raider gestured to his chest and arm. "I mean, with all the wizards tossing spells around, it's not like someone won't see it."

He shrugged. "It'll just be another artifact as far as everyone else is concerned."

"Then we should get going. The AET needs our help."

James pushed off the pillar and walked toward his truck. "Yeah, let's get going. I've still got some anger to work off."

Shay shook her head.

Those motherfuckers better hope they don't say anything about Alison.

MICHAEL ANDERLE

The Professor offered the familiar elf across the table in the back of the Leanan Sídhe a smile.

"You're coming here so often lately, Correk, that some might consider you a regular."

The elf chuckled. "What can I say? I go where the trouble is."

The air shimmered around them, and the sounds of the rest of the bar died away. They'd be able to have a private conversation now even without the Professor taking any precautions. Always a nice bonus of being old friends with the Fixer.

"To what do I owe the pleasure tonight?" the Professor asked.

Correk folded his hands in front of him. "I've been looking into the list of objects stolen from the museum." His expression darkened, and he reached into his pocket. He pulled out a piece of paper and slid it over to the Professor. "Before I become worried, I think the best thing would be for you to let me know what has been recovered. My concerns may be unwarranted."

The Professor pulled a pen out of his pocket and starting skimming down the list checking off objects. "Between the police, Miz Carson, and James, we've collected the bulk of the objects. I think the thieves were overconfident. Maybe they would have been able to elude Miz Carson by herself or James by himself, but those two together are a frightening combination, especially working with the LAPD."

Correk gave him a quick nod. "There's some impressive

and unusual magic being used to shield the objects. Whoever is behind this isn't just some group of common criminals looking to make a quick buck. I wouldn't be surprised if they hadn't somehow pulled the strings to get those objects displayed at the museum."

The Professor continued reading and checking off artifacts. "Aye, I don't doubt it. If this were any other city but LA they might have gotten away with it." He picked up his beer to take a sip. "Stupidity or arrogance." He shrugged.

A waitress approached the table. She didn't seem to notice when she stepped past the sound barrier. She smiled at Correk. "Can I get you anything, sir?"

The elf nodded at the Professor's glass. "I'll have what he's having."

"Right away." She headed toward the bar.

The Professor set down his beer. "Even if someone powerful is behind this, I doubt they'd be so sloppy as to leave an easy path from their pawns to them. We both know how that goes."

Correk frowned. "If we just take a few of them alive, that might help. There are certain spells I might be able to use."

The other man shook his head. "From what Miz Carson told me, the lad is on the warpath now, and the police aren't exactly any calmer. The criminals seem unwilling to surrender while breathing as well. I think we'll have to be satisfied with recovering the artifacts."

He finished checking the list and pushed it over. The waitress returned with a beer for Correk and set it down in front of him before heading off.

The elf took a sip as he looked down the list. After a

minute, he sighed and shook his head. "I remember when I first came to Earth, I thought a single murder investigation was complicated. Now that kind of problem seems quaint."

The Professor arched a brow. "Find something you don't like?"

Correk tapped several of the non-checked items. "According to the museum, most of these are minor artifacts, barely better than toys. And they are, to the untrained person, but if you know the proper incantations and unlocking magic or if you're willing to make the proper sacrifices, they're much more powerful."

"Sacrifices? Should I be taking that literally, old friend?"

The Fixer nodded slowly. "Lives, limbs. In one case, souls even. A lot of these are much more valuable than anyone has realized, and far more dangerous. The Bowl of the Winds is a difficult-to-use artifact, almost not worth the trouble, but most of these aren't that difficult and don't require as much power. Just knowledge and ruthlessness." He shook his head. "No wonder they didn't care about the circlet. It's another thing that's hard to use."

The Professor shrugged. "If the museum didn't know, maybe the thieves don't."

"The thieves may or may not know, but if there is someone behind them, they *definitely* know." He tapped the paper. "The pattern's clear. Most of the artifacts of real concern haven't been recovered, which means they divided up the artifacts based on at least some criteria and knowledge."

"Then I suppose all we can do now is sit back and hope Miz Carson and James recover them. They are on their way to what should be the last collection of stolen artifacts." He picked up his drink. "This feels like a night where a few more drinks are in order."

Correk chuckled. "Is there ever a night where that's not the case for you?"

"No, and I wouldn't want to live in such a world."

"You should take care. We have miles to go before our work is finished."

The Professor smiled. "Don't worry, Correk. I'm not checking out of this war so soon."

Three helicopters zoomed toward Mar Vista. Even though all the men on her strike team fit into the two choppers, she'd made sure to load more than a few toys on the third helicopter.

Yeah, all that budget shit goes away after a cop gets killed. Maybe if we'd had anti-magic bullets at that battle, Johnson would still be alive.

A squadron of rocket drones trailed along in loose formation. She would have preferred to control them on site, but she had good men back at the station who were too banged up to come along but not too hurt to control a drone watching over them. It'd still be AET watching out for AET, with a little help from a man who was a force of nature.

I hated you for a long time, Brownstone, because I thought you were too powerful and you caused too much collateral damage, but now I'm depending on that. Hell, you help us pull this off, I'll see to it that department insurance covers all those cars that got shot up in the parking garage. I need your power now.

"Touchdown in five minutes, Lieutenant," the pilot relayed.

"Good. Time to end this shit."

"Don't just stand there, you morons," Logan shouted to the assembled men. "Get ready. The cops are on their way now, and probably Brownstone, too."

One of the men frowned. "Why aren't we just getting the fuck out of here if we know they're coming?"

Logan shook his head. "It's too late. I don't know how they found us, but they did. We stand and fight. We take revenge for all the guys that Brownstone and the cops have killed. We have the advantage, though. This isn't a handful of guys on a road. We're assembled here in force, and we know they're coming. We're going to kill Brownstone and every last cop who comes at us, and show them our power."

The men cheered.

"Now get to it," he shouted.

The men scrambled toward the vans. Several boxes of minor artifacts for their use lay inside, and even if every man wasn't a wizard or Oriceran, they could fight like one. This time, the cops and Brownstone wouldn't have complete surprise and overwhelming strength on their side. It'd be an even fight, one Logan intended to win.

I'll show Tak what kind of man I am.

He marched to a side office and threw open the door. A large box lay on the ground with several artifacts inside. He picked up two gauntlets—one gold, the other silver—and slipped them on. Warmth shot through his body, and he took a deep breath.

The man turned, grinned, and smashed his fist into a wooden desk. The force of the blow split it down the center, and it collapsed in on itself.

He raised the golden gauntlet and uttered the dwarven word for "pain."

A massive fireball blasted from the gauntlet and hit the wall, blowing out a huge chunk and leaving the wall smoldering.

He snorted. "Let's see how you like taking that to the face, Brownstone."

Logan headed over to the box and pulled out two crystal rings. He slipped one on each hand over the gauntlets. One would protect him from magic, the other from conventional forces.

He didn't spend a lot of time paying attention to Brownstone, but everything he'd heard suggested the guy was strong and durable, not that he liked to throw spells. The AET mostly relied on conventional weapons with magical defenses. He'd have to be careful about anti-magic bullets, but the fact that one of his teams had injured a large chunk of the AET proved the ammo was in short supply.

Logan shook his head. Sometimes he let himself forget

that his work wasn't just about collecting money. Even if he was on the bottom, he was part of a powerful organization. It didn't matter that he didn't know their ultimate plans. It only mattered that he'd be on the winning side of something he was sure would change Earth more than the truth about Oriceran coming out.

Every instinct told him so, and this was his chance to prove himself to those above him.

"We'll do this. We'll win and prove to Tak and his bosses who the real power in LA is. Bring it on, Brownstone. You're coming here to die."

The AET team disembarked and everyone ran to the cargo helicopter to pull off some of the additional gear, including a couple of railguns and rocket launchers. With their thick black armor and helmets with red goggles, they looked more like angry robots arming for an uprising than police.

Maria nodded, satisfied. It was time to kick ass.

Tactical drones bearing rockets circled overhead. This situation had turned into a war zone, and she intended to win.

The lieutenant cleared her throat. "This is Hall to all drone teams. I want you on standby. Going to surprise those motherfuckers when the time is right." She gestured to two officers holding railguns. "Same thing with you two. We're fielding a small team because of all the injuries, so we need to play it right. Jacobs, get that turret set up ASAP. I want to test their lead allergies."

The officer nodded and hurried over to the large black case containing the heavy turret.

A few gawkers stood on the street.

"You!" she yelled at them. "Get the hell out of here unless you want to get caught in a major firefight."

The people turned and ran in the opposite direction.

She turned back to her target, a large and allegedly abandoned warehouse. Their tactical drones had already taken out the surveillance drones the criminals had up, but the enemy might have magical surveillance methods. No one had tried to make a break for it.

Ready to stand and fight, huh? Good for you, shit stains. You had to go and make me very, very mad, and now I'm going to give you one chance to give up before I deliver the pain.

Sirens sang in the distance. Good. They'd need the other cops to control the perimeter.

A familiar F-350 turned the corner and screeched to a halt. James and Shay hopped out of the vehicle. The tomb raider spent a moment digging in the back seat and slipping small objects into her tactical harness.

Brownstone was grim-faced even for him as he marched toward Maria.

"They try to run yet?" he asked.

Maria tapped her wrist control to switch on her external transmit mode and shook her head. "Nope. They're still holed up in there. We've seen some movement from windows, but no one has come out. Think they're waiting for us."

"Good," the bounty hunter rumbled.

Several AET officers set metal cubes down on the ground and pressed buttons on the tops. They expanded into tactical shields. Soon, they had a nice portable line of defense set up. They might not be able to take magic, but they could take a large-caliber rifle round.

Police cars and vans pulled in, and officers hurried out as more and more arrived. Maria ignored them. The chief had already delivered the orders. AET would go in with the support of Brownstone. The other officers would maintain the perimeter and provide general outside fire support.

Several cops started setting up spotlights.

Maria waited until Shay wandered over, decked out in a utility belt and tactical harness filled with everything from knives to grenades. She and Brownstone had two separate holsters and multiple mags. They were practically an AET team in and of themselves.

She nodded at Brownstone. "Let's see if our boys inside want to do the smart thing."

He grunted. "I hope not."

"Yeah, honestly, I hope not, too."

Maria activated the loudspeaker mode in her helmet. All the power of yelling, none of the strain.

"This is the LAPD. We have you surrounded. You are to come out unarmed, and with your hands up. If you do so your safety can be guaranteed, but any sudden movements will be considered hostile actions, and you will be fired upon. This is your final warning."

A gunshot rang out and bounced off Maria's thick black armor with a spark. She sighed and shook her head. She ducked behind one of the shields and switched to an AET frequency.

The lieutenant readied the rifle. "Good. Just the answer

I was hoping for. McMahon, knock on their front door for me."

The AET officer hoisted a rocket launcher onto his shoulder. "Backblast area clear," he shouted. The rocket roared toward the aluminum loading bay door.

23

The door exploded in a ball of fire and smoke, and metal and wood rained from the sky. Fireballs, bullets, and a rainbow of different-colored energy bolts shot from the warehouse. Dozens of men lay in wait inside in a maze of crates and boxes.

Multiple enemies. Kill, the amulet whispered.

That's the plan, James thought back

Advancing behind cover, AET opened up with their rifles, only with lethal ammo this time. McMahon loaded another rocket and demonstrated his fine skill in knocking out walls with high explosives.

James and Shay both fired, but their weapons were drowned out as every non-AET cop outside opened up on the warehouse. A criminal at a window was dumb enough to pop up. A SWAT sniper emptied out his head a second later.

The AET squad broke into two teams of three, using their shields on both sides, along with the rain of bullets from all the officers behind them, to cover their advance.

The two railgun officers knelt and readied their weapons, poking the barrels through small ports in their shields.

Jacobs' turret came online, the heavy machine gun bursting to life and sweeping back and forth. Several thugs all but exploded in a red mist as the bullets ripped into them.

James narrowed his eyes. Men were dying, and they weren't accomplishing much in taking down cops, but not enough criminals were dying for his taste or that of his amulet. Several men stood directly in the open, firing with abandon either with guns or wands, but the police bullets bounced off them, disappeared, melted, or changed direction.

The bounty hunter nodded to Shay and pointed to a side door. "Let's go that way. We can flank them and stay out of the cops' way."

She nodded back, and both ducked and broke away from the AET team they'd been trailing.

Bullets whizzed by James, a few striking him. They stung but didn't do much to slow him down. He glanced over his shoulder. Shay hadn't used any new defensive artifact. Given what they'd already seen, she would need to be careful.

The AET frontline squads had advanced almost to the open door on either side. James and Shay moved around the corner.

The bounty hunter kicked in a side door, wood splintering everywhere. He charged toward the battle site and turned a corner to run into two men with wands.

James didn't bother to shoot them. He threw his gun at them instead and charged. A shoulder check sent one of the wizards into the wall. His opponent chanted a spell in some language James didn't recognize, and a swirling round blue shield appeared in front of him.

The bounty hunter grabbed the neck of the other one and snapped it in one fluid motion.

He picked the man up and tossed him at his friend. The body bounced off a shield with a blue flash.

Shay ran toward him, unsheathed her sword, and stabbed through the shield in one fluid motion. She yanked the blade out and smirked as her victim fell to the ground. She sheathed the weapon and grabbed her adamantine knives, having retrieved the blade from Brownstone after the previous fight.

The echo of gunshots bounced around the small hallway, and then a huge explosion shook the building. The roar of a railgun followed, and James and Shay turned the corner just in time to see a man reduced to paste through the power of lethally applied science.

Four men near the hallway turned toward James, their hands glowing.

"Any of you the fucker in charge?" the bounty hunter rumbled.

The men yelled and charged. James met their charge with a punch to one, an elbow to another, and a knee to a third. The three men flew backward, one smashing into a wall.

The fourth man tried to flank James, but Shay stabbed him in the neck with one knife before spinning and disemboweling him with the other. She didn't wait to soak in the victory. The tomb raider charged the man stuck in the wall and perforated him.

The bounty hunter stomped toward the two surviving men. They'd hopped back up and were shaking their heads. One threw a punch, and James caught the man's hand with his fist.

"Was that supposed to hurt?" The bounty hunter squeezed until the bones cracked. The man fell to his knees, and a powerful direct punch from the bounty hunter snapped the man's head back. He fell to the floor, dead.

The remaining man shook his head. "You'll fucking pay for that, Brownstone." He lifted his hands, and they burst into flames. He grinned.

James didn't charge Flame Hands. He stalked toward him like a beast. "Sure, asshole."

The amulet whispered about killing in James' mind, all the way beaming its joy over the destruction to its partner.

AET had breached the front door with five officers led by Lieutenant Hall. Their shields had been shredded, and several had holes in their armor. They sprinted for cover behind the piles of crates filling the warehouse.

As beat up as they were, half the enemy force already lay dead or dying.

The police heavy machine gun had gone silent, but a railgun shot through with a roar and blew the leg off an elf who had been tossing green energy bolts.

The bounty hunter finished his approach on his opponent. "I'll give one free punch," he growled. "After that, you die, motherfucker."

James held up a hand to stop Shay from rushing the man.

Sometimes you had to make life complicated to make your point.

Flame Hands threw a punch right at James' face. The bounty hunter didn't block or dodge. He grunted as the man impacted his face, the flame and force of the blow barely stinging.

Old forces, the amulet whispered. *Already adapted. Kill enemy. Useless sample.*

"I agree," James muttered. He snapped his hand out and grabbed the man's neck, squeezing.

The man gasped for breath as the bounty hunter marched over to the wall. He smashed the man's head against the wall until the thug's battered face was almost unrecognizable. James dropped the man to the ground.

Shay jogged up to his side. "Next time, don't be cute about it. Just let me stab the fucker."

James shrugged. "I wanted to make a point."

She snorted. "To who? By the time this is over they'll all be dead."

The bounty grunted. "Yeah. Guess you're right."

He pulled out a frag grenade and tossed it toward a group of riflemen hiding behind some crates. They tried to scatter but didn't make it far enough before the grenade shredded them.

A wizard advanced on the AET on the other end of the warehouse, their bullets bouncing off his skin. He raised his wand, and twelve flaming arrows appeared. They fell in a shower, each exploding. The armored cops flew back but quickly recovered. A few staggered, bleeding from some of their open wounds.

"Fuck," James yelled. "Even with their anti-magic

deflectors, they won't last long. We need to close the gap and fuck up that wizard."

Three men popped up from behind another crate, two elves and a human, each holding a crossbow. James had spotted the weapons blasting out purple bolts earlier.

Another railgun round blasted into the warehouse and slammed into a thug covered in black scales. His magical armor didn't do much to protect him from the hyper-velocity round. His body, complete with a new gaping hole, flew back until it crashed into a wall.

James took advantage of the distraction of the shot to charge into the thug trio.

One of the elves got off a shot and pierced James' shoulder. He grunted at the pain but still closed on the men. He snatched the magical crossbow out of the elf's hand and brained him with it. With a quick flick of the wrist, he shoved a knife into the throat of the other elf.

Before James could turn on the human, Shay slit the man's throat from behind. She sheathed her knives and pulled out what looked like a small marble.

The tomb raider sighed. "Do you have any idea how much this thing costs?"

James pulled the knife out of the dead elf. "More than a good meal at Jessie Rae's?"

"Yeah. A lot more."

He pointed to the wizard pinning down the AET. "Maybe Maria will reimburse you."

Shay grinned. "I can hope."

The tomb raider shook the marble for several seconds and threw it straight toward the wizard.

"Fall back," Maria shouted. The damned wizard whipped his wand around, and a dozen new flaming arrows winked into existence. They all shot toward the AET, each exploding. The shockwave sent the team sprawling, their anti-magic deflectors darkening. She'd gotten every man a new one, but the artifacts were still almost at their limits.

On the other end of the warehouse, James and Shay were working their way through the enemy, which at least helped take the pressure off Maria's team. The tomb raider wound her arm up and threw something tiny toward the wizard.

What the fuck is that?

The lieutenant didn't have time to even begin to process the possibilities when Shay's projectile slammed into the wizard. A loud buzz filled the air, and the man's skin turned to stone. A few seconds later, he exploded. Bits of stony wizard rained down for the next several seconds.

Maria shook her head. "Okay, that was different. Come on, men. I think we've thinned out the normal guys. Swap in the good stuff." She ejected her magazine and put in a magazine filled with anti-magic bullets.

I'll probably be paying Dannec off for the next five years after this fight, but I don't care.

A man in a pendant popped up from behind a crate, grenade launcher in hand. Maria had unloaded a normal magazine into him earlier to no effect.

She aimed her rifle and fired, and he jerked back and dropped his weapon. Another two bullets put him down.

Damned expensive way to kill a man, but it got the job done.

The AET rushed forward, mowing down several thugs who'd proven resistant to everything but railgun fire and heavy machine guns before.

Brownstone and Shay swept in from the side. The tomb raider was slicing and dicing man after man. The bounty hunter didn't even bother with a weapon half the time, though he occasionally tossed a grenade.

He was taking bullets, fireballs, and all sorts of magical blasts and barely flinching. A few burns and cuts here and there, but nothing serious.

Damn, Brownstone, what kind of magic you using?

A wizard in the corner raised his wand. A swirling kaleidoscopic portal winked into existence behind him, and several men rushed out, followed by a Kilomea, all circled by pulsating orbs.

Maria did a double-take. "A Kilomea? What the fuck is up with this gang?" She shook her head. "Take down that wizard."

The AET crossfire created a few new holes in the wizard. He fell face-forward, and his portal closed just as another man was stepping through. Only the front half of him made it.

The new arrivals glanced at the dead wizard and the bisected man before raising their palms, the orbs floating around them spinning faster.

"Incoming, take cover," Maria shouted.

A volley of fireballs shot from the men and exploded around the AET, sending them sprawling to the ground. Maria hissed at the pain. Her deflector was getting danger-ously dark, as were her men's. One or two more good hits would shatter them.

The lieutenant pushed herself to her feet, just in time to receive a backhand from the charging Kilomea. The cop crashed into several crates, which toppled down on her.

Fuck. That hurt.

The hulking Kilomea slammed another man hard against the wall before a well-timed railgun blast from outside vaporized most of his upper body.

Maria crawled from under the crates, a throbbing ache in every part of her body. She grabbed her rifle and aimed at the reinforcements. A semi-translucent wall of flame floated a few feet in front of them.

She fired a few rounds, but her bullets melted when they hit the flame. The enemies, their faces tight, responded with another batch of fireballs. The crates and boxes the AET were using for cover blew apart.

Maria grabbed the man the Kilomea had hurled against the door by the arms and started dragging him back toward the entrance, doing her best to ignore her pain. She might hurt, but she'd obviously not broken anything.

She sent the message, "Fall back."

The screams of dying men and the roars of explosions echoed down the hallway as Logan leaned against the wall. The sacrifice of some of the men was necessary. Part of winning a battle was waiting for the proper time and place.

He'd also not been completely honest with the men. The most important artifacts were still in the SUV. The transfer would be complete soon, and the longer they held the attention of the police at the warehouse, the safer those artifacts would be.

Every operation had different ways to fail, but if they could at least assure the delivery of the artifacts in the SUV, there was still some hope they could call this situation a success.

A series of explosions shook the warehouse.

Logan's phone chimed with a text, and he pulled it out of his pocket.

Delivered

Logan nodded and spun around the corner. He raised the golden gauntlet and squinted. The black-armored AET were in the distance, retreating, from what he could tell. The sacrifices were over. It was time for victory.

24

James frowned as Maria pulled her team back. He pulled out a frag grenade and hurled it toward the men advancing behind the flame shield. It exploded. The men stumbled back, shielded from the shrapnel but not the shockwave.

"You fuckers should have taken my surrender offer," Maria shouted. "Now it's time for a little backup."

The AET team had retreated all the way to the entrance.

James looked at her, confused. From what Shay had told him, she barely had enough healthy guys to scrape together her entrance team, and sending in normal cops would lead to a slaughter.

"Fuck it," James muttered. "My amulet can take flame. I'm gonna charge them."

Shay shook her head. "You don't have any idea if that's normal flame. Bad fucking idea and… What the hell is that noise?"

A buzzing hum grew closer as the rocket-carrying

drones flew in through the burned-out hole where the main door used to stand. Once inside, the drones flew higher and angled down. Dozens of rockets blasted from the squadron of machines. It was time to rain down a little summary judgment.

The new arrivals' fire shield didn't extend more than a few feet above them. Rocket after rocket pounded into them until there was nothing but the charred remains of what used to be men surrounded by burning debris.

A massive fireball zipped out of an open hallway and hit the ground close to Maria's team, and the explosion sent the cops flying. One man's anti-magic deflector shattered as he hit the ground.

New enemy, the amulet whispered. *New adaptation. Grow stronger.*

A tall man in silver and gold gauntlets emerged from the hallway, and the AET opened fire. He gritted his teeth as the bullets struck him, but he didn't go down.

Shay shook her head. "Shit. Never expected to see him here."

James looked at her. "Who the fuck is he?"

"Logan Smith."

"Killer?"

Shay nodded. "Good, but not spectacular. Looks like he's moved up in the world."

James grunted. "Time to move him back down to where he belongs."

One of the AET officers grabbed a wounded and unconscious man and pulled him back toward the main line of police. The four remaining officers kept up their fire, but Logan was barely moving.

The drones above unloaded the remainder of their rockets, surrounding the man in a cloud of burning death and destruction.

"Did they get him?"

The AET officers stopped firing, waiting for the smoke to clear. When it did, James narrowed his eyes.

Logan stood there, barely scratched, and his clothes hardly mussed. He raised his golden gauntlet and muttered something, and another fireball flew toward the AET. Maria's team managed to jump out of the way, but the explosion again sent them careening through the air, with several of their deflectors shattering. They ducked behind the remnants of some crates.

The criminal lifted his arm, and fireballs started blasting drones out of the sky. The remaining ones dropped and flew toward the exit, but the criminal leader destroyed several more before the rest escaped. He chuckled at the withdrawal of the drones before blasting another fireball at the AET officers creeping around the corner.

"A little help, Brownstone," Maria shouted.

The amulet shot a spurt of joy into the bounty hunter's thoughts that he could only think of as a giggle.

Fight the enemy. Kill the enemy. Grow stronger.

Shay and James both crouched. Logan surveyed the area with a smirk on his face.

The tomb raider shook her head. "What's the plan? We need to get out there and take that guy down. These assholes have been tough, but this guy seems even tougher. Logan's obviously the guy calling the shots."

James frowned and looked at the AET officer still

pulling his wounded friend back toward the main police line.

Whispy Doom, James thought.

Improper name.

Like I give a fuck. You're liking this shit, right?

Kill the enemy. Grow stronger.

You want me to do that, you need to help me keep Shay from moving. You can do more than I've been using you for, so I know you can do this shit.

Touch target.

James' right hand twitched, and he leaned toward the tomb raider. "Not you," he rumbled, and touched her legs.

Shay's eyes widened, and she fell back. "I can't…move my legs. What the fuck did you do?"

He shook his head. "Even the cops with their armor and deflectors are getting fucked up. I'm ending this shit, and this asshole."

"Release me from whatever the fuck it is that you did to me," Shay hissed.

James shook his head and looked at the smirking Logan. The earlier thug had made the risk of being a Brownstone clear. Alison's face had been splashed all over the world. Every time the bounty hunter took a job, he'd need to make sure he did whatever was needed to ensure no one would threaten her.

The thugs had threatened Shay and Alison, and they'd killed a cop. He clenched his teeth. This shit needed to end.

Yes, the amulet whispered. *Anger. Hatred. Sufficient power.*

"That fucker is mine," James growled. "I've got protection, but you used up your angel ring, and I'm not letting anyone take what is mine from me." Tendrils burst from the amulet and expanded into armor across his chest and back, visible through some of the holes in his shirt. No weapon appeared.

"Let me go, James," Shay shouted.

The bounty hunter shook his head and stood. "Smith," he shouted, and took a step toward Logan. "Are you in charge of all the fuckers we just killed?"

The other man sneered at Brownstone. "You're gonna pay for all those men you killed, Brownstone."

"Your men have threatened my family twice now, Smith," the bounty hunter rumbled. "Some shit I can't let slide."

"Fuck your family, Brownstone. Don't worry, I'll pay them a visit after I'm finished with you." Logan raised his gauntlet and grinned. He muttered something under his breath, and a massive fireball screamed toward James.

Kill the enemy. Defeat the enemy.

The fireball exploded around James, and Logan threw his head back and laughed. The bounty hunter ignored the slight pain and continued stomping toward the other man, his shirt now incinerated, and the armor obvious.

Logan kept laughing for several seconds before glancing toward James. His eyes widened. "What the fuck?"

The bounty hunter continued advancing on the man, death in his eyes.

Maria motioned her men back. "Oh, fuck, move back. Everyone retreat, and move the fuck back from Brownstone."

Logan launched another fireball directly into James and then another, but the bounty hunter kept moving forward, one slow step at a time. By the time James stood in front of him, the other man was panting and shaking his head.

The criminal let out a nervous laugh. "So you have magic armor. Big fucking deal. Fireballs aren't my only tricks. Die, Brownstone!"

He swung a fist at James' face. The bounty hunter blocked the blow with ease and slammed his fist into Logan's face.

The man stumbled back and shook his head to clear it. "Impossible. You shouldn't be able to get through my shield."

James grunted and delivered a vicious combo. Blood fountained from Logan's broken nose. The bounty hunter caught the criminal's arm as he attempted a feeble punch. With a quick bend, the arm snapped in two. Logan howled in pain and fell to his knees.

The amulet radiated joy and satisfaction. Few real thoughts passed through James' head, only the anger and the bloodthirst.

James put his hands on the sides of Logan's head. "You fuckers came into my town. You stole from a museum. You kidnapped my girlfriend. You killed a cop, and you fucking threatened my daughter. You think I'm gonna let that shit slide? You think I'm gonna let anyone threaten my little girl?"

A sickening crunch filled the air as the bounty hunter tightened his grip and ripped the man's head clean off. He tossed the trophy to the side and then slammed his boot into the headless body, sending it flying into a wall.

He growled and slowly looked around, his breathing

labored. Dozens of dead thugs lay on the ground, but he wasn't satisfied. More. He needed more enemies to kill.

Shay shook out her legs. "Finally." She shot to her feet and ran over to James. "I'll deal with that little trick later, but I love you."

James snapped his head toward her, anger still clouding his mind and the amulet whispering.

Anger. Hate. Sufficient power. Stronger enemies defeated.

Shay held her hands in front of her. "I love you, James. I'm safe. Alison's safe. Everyone's safe. It's all over. The criminals are all dead."

He stared at her for a moment, still breathing hard. James blinked, and some of the hatred slid away. The armor retracted.

"You with me, baby?" Shay whispered.

James took a deep breath and nodded. "Yeah. I'm with you."

Twenty minutes later, the warehouse was filled with uniformed officers looking through crates and backrooms, and cataloging bodies. The burned-out wreck of the main warehouse resembled a plane crash site more than the location of a police shootout.

Maria made her way back inside. Although more of her men had gotten banged up, this time it was nothing serious. She was more than a little sore, but the painkillers were hiding it well enough.

She spotted Shay in the corner talking to an officer. Brownstone stood by himself down the hallway, frowning.

Yeah. After what I just saw, I think I'll leave him be for now. I wanted to unleash the beast, and I got exactly that.

The AET lieutenant made her way over to Shay as the other officer departed.

Maria cleared her throat. "Still cataloging crap, but even ignoring all the artifacts on those guy's bodies, there's a bunch of stuff in some back rooms. No one was seriously injured on the good guys' team."

Shay chuckled and rubbed her neck. "I'm more of a gray gal than a good guy."

The cop shrugged. "Whatever." She nodded toward Brownstone. "What the hell was that?"

The tomb raider furrowed her brow. "What do you mean? His armor?"

Obvious concern radiated off Shay.

Maria sighed. "I don't give a shit about whatever magic armor he was using if that's what you're worried about. I've always assumed he used more than a few artifacts. No one's that badass naturally."

"What are you asking about, then?"

A look of relief spread over Shay's face, and Maria's cop instincts almost made her want to ask more about the armor, but she decided against it.

"I've seen him beat down people before, some pretty viciously, like King Pyro." Maria shook her head. "But he was operating on a whole other level of anger there. I mean, he ripped a guy's head off, for crying out loud."

Shay sighed. "These guys threatened to hurt Alison. It...pushed him over the edge. That's also why he beat down King Pyro. He did the same sort of thing. James redefines overprotective. I don't know how we got through that trial without him throwing the other lawyer through a wall."

The cop slowly nodded. "I feel sorry for anyone who tries to date her, and her trying to date anyone."

The tomb raider snorted. "The little princess has James wrapped around her finger. She knows how to handle her big, overprotective daddy over there. It's when someone else is threatening her." She sighed. "Or me. That's when James loses his temper."

Maria looked back at Brownstone. "That why you stayed out of it?"

A hint of something crossed Shay's face, but the cop couldn't quite identify it.

Shay shrugged. "James told me to stay back, and I couldn't argue with him at the time."

"You let him tell you what to do? You don't seem like the type."

The tomb raider smirked, but after a moment she sighed. "No, really, I couldn't argue. He...did something to freeze my legs. He didn't want me in the way when he took that asshole out."

Maria frowned. "'Did something?' Magic?"

"Something like that." Shay chuckled.

"What's so funny?"

The tomb raider pointed at James. "These assholes just kept riling him up by threatening me and then Alison. The criminals should have just kept their mouths shut, especially about his daughter. They might have stood a better chance that way."

Maria nodded and looked at James and Shay. "I know you joked about the lawyer, but what do you seriously think would have happened if the government had blocked his adoption?"

Shay let out a long sigh. "I'm not sure, but let's just say that if Alison didn't want to leave James and both of them decided to stand their ground, a lot of people might be dead. And those two, and I, would be somewhere else."

Maria patted her on the back. "Well, I'm glad you're here, Shay." She smirked. "I should go to museums with you more often. Seems like they're more interesting than I ever would have guessed."

The two women shared a chuckle.

Tak sighed and leaned back in his chair. Logan'd had his faults, but the man and those under him had been very useful for jobs and the cause in general. The loss of trained men and artifacts was devastating, but he would explain it to the Council somehow. He just had to think of the right angle.

"The most important artifacts made it through. I'm sure that if I tell them, they'll understand."

"No, we won't," a hollow, raspy voice whispered in his ear. "But thank you for your service."

The dwarf's heart galloped. He spun in his seat, but his head melted before he could turn around.

Smite-Williams sat at his desk, a bottle of beer in front of him as he looked down the list. They'd recovered ninety percent of the artifacts, but several of those that concerned Correk hadn't been found. Now, with all the thieves dead, there wasn't anyone to question.

The old man let out a long sigh. He'd been in the fight against the darkness for too long to begrudge a partial victory.

He took a long draw from his beer. "Whoever is behind this took a hell of a bloody nose. Good enough for now. No point in bothering the lad and Miz Carson to go looking for something that's long gone. I'll enjoy my half-loaf."

"Watch the wood," James reminded. "Watch your meat."

He had to admire the focus of the Camp Brownstone men. They'd managed to keep their attention on the barbeque pit despite the thousands of people milling around the area, and dozens surrounding their tent.

Shorty laughed. "I don't think the police want us watching our meat in public. Ain't that right, Sergeant Mack?"

Mack snorted and shook his head from at the other end of the pit. "There are kids in the crowd. Keep it PG, Shorty."

"I ain't say nothing nasty. You're the one with the dirty mind."

The men all laughed.

James grinned and shook his head. He looked at the bounty hunters crowded around the pit, with the various smaller groups responsible for monitoring the progress on the different meats being cooked. It was a solid group of men united in the cause of good food, not violence.

A light breeze blew in with the scent of salt from the clear blue ocean water visible in the distance. Two palm trees even provided a bit of shelter from the sun. It was a perfect little slice of barbeque paradise.

Various other teams were all over the area with their own tents, but the mob around Team Brownstone filled James with confidence. People seemed to be enjoying the food as much as his notoriety.

This shit is going down even better than I planned. No one's bitching, and all the barbeque freaks look happy.

James smiled as Lachlan peered at some chicken and flipped it over. A lot of the guys were still waiting for their boss to give them direct orders, but the young hothead seemed to really get into the cooking himself once they had arrived at the Turf and Surf BBQ Championship.

"Develop good pitmaster skills," James explained, "and you'll have something to fall back on if you ever get sick of being a bounty hunter."

The men all laughed.

Trey, Isaiah, and Max stood behind tables handing out food to guests. Their quick hands passed the stiff paper plates filled with meat and sides to hungry-looking people.

A leggy redhead in a sundress sauntered up to the tent and beamed a smile at Trey. "This is the Brownstone Agency team, right?" she purred.

Trey grinned. "You're right about that, ma'am. I can assure you we take barbeque as seriously as we do bounty hunting, and we're good at both." He bowed with his arm beneath his chest.

The woman giggled. "I can only imagine. You strike me as the kind of men who are good at...everything." She fluttered her eyelashes. "Would you say that's true?"

He shrugged and winked. "Never had any complaints."

James smirked but didn't say anything.

Wish Shay hadn't needed to hit that tomb raid. I think she would have liked this. Or shit, maybe it's still too much for her to be around all these people as herself. Too bad Royce's old CO's retirement party was today. He would have loved to see the guys hanging out together in a different way.

The bounty hunter looked around. He was surrounded by good friends, but he had particularly wanted to share his joy in the event with his girlfriend and the Marine responsible for turning a bunch of gangbangers into barbeque-slinging bounty hunters.

James might have given the boys the chance, but Royce had given them the discipline to make their dream come true.

A white-haired man in an expensive suit wandered up to James, snapping him out of his thoughts. "Good afternoon, Mr. Brownstone."

The bounty hunter managed not to grunt. "Yeah. Good afternoon."

"Arthur." The man extended his hand.

The bounty hunter gave it a firm but not too strong shake. "Guess you already know who I am."

Arthur smirked. "Yes. You are rather famous, or infamous, depending on how we look at things."

"So, how do you look at things?"

The man shrugged. "I think you're an interesting fellow in either event. You've lived such a colorful life, after all, and dealt with villains most of us can only imagine." He laughed. "When I was a young boy, I used to think about what it'd be like to live in a world of powerful men and women fighting other powerful men and women. I must say, it ended up far more prosaically than I would have imagined. I suppose that's just more proof that people can adapt to anything. I'm sure you have many fascinating stories, though."

Here it came.

James sighed. "Go ahead, then. Might as well get this over with."

"Go ahead?" The man tilted his head, a confused look on his face. "I'm afraid I'm not following you, Mr. Brownstone."

"I'm sure you have all sorts of questions about bounties I've gone after. That sort of sh...stuff." James shrugged. "I can't spend all day talking about it, but I'll give you a few minutes if you can narrow down what you're interested in. I don't really want to talk about the Drow, though. Do you have questions about anything other than the Drow?"

Arthur laughed. "Most assuredly."

James nodded. "Fine. As long as they aren't about the Drow."

"They aren't even about your more violent day job." The man nodded at the pit. "Last time I checked, this was a barbeque competition, not a bounty-hunting competition."

"Yeah, that it is." James chuckled and shrugged, some of the tension leaving his shoulders and neck. He was glad someone remembered that he was there as a pitmaster and not a bounty hunter.

Arthur leaned closer and lowered his voice conspiratorially. "With that elf girl becoming such a big name in barbeque, it has made me consider other alternatives on Earth. I realize that I've been closeminded these last few decades, and I despair over that. Accordingly, I've decided to expand my horizons."

"How so?"

The man gestured with a flourish. "By exploring the glories of the barbeque of the Far East."

James furrowed his brow. "You mean like *yakiniku*?"

The man shook his head. "Close. I'm talking more about *bulgogi*. Have you ever had it? Korean barbeque? I've just really gotten into it this last year, which is ironic because I've been to Seoul several times and never had it. I've made them hire a Korean bulgogi chef at my country club. The man is a wizard." He frowned. "Well, not a *literal* wizard, but if you'd had some of his beef, you might believe he is."

James nodded. "Sounds great. I've had a decent amount of it, but nowhere near enough to call myself an expert. I can appreciate different flavor profiles, but it's not like Korean barbeque ends with beef. They manage to hit all the major meats, just like American barbeque. Some things are universal, like the most delicious animals."

Arthur rubbed his chin. "You're more well-informed than I expected."

The bounty hunter chuckled, not sure if he should be insulted.

"Of course, of course," the older man continued. "I suppose I've fallen in love with some aspects of Korean barbeque because cooking it can be a little easier than some forms of American barbeque. Fewer arguments about low and slow and all that, you know? I'm far more interested in the seasoning than the cooking."

"Yeah, I get that. It's all what you want to get out of it." He nodded toward some brisket on the pit being monitored by TJ. "I want to master one style of barbeque before I even think about trying to go on to something else, and there are just so many options in American barbeque. I can't even begin to think about trying to hit up all the options in Korean barbeque. Or Japanese, or Nigerian, or whatever.

Arthur eyed Lachlan as he set some chicken on a plate. "Of course, Mr. Brownstone. I admire your desire for thorough mastery of your current craft." He licked his lips. "If you'll excuse me, though, I think I need to compare your chicken against the last Korean barbequed chicken I ate."

"Yeah, sure."

Arthur wandered toward Trey, Isaiah, and Max as James smiled.

He grinned. A rich guy, a bounty hunter, ex-gang members, a cop, and countless others. Barbeque crossed all boundaries.

The woman maneuvered through a roped-off area for the elite patrons, checking her headscarf to make sure her hair was still concealed. The wealthy chatted, either standing or reclining in beach chairs as waiters with trays of drinks traveled from person to person.

A perky blonde smiled when she spotted the woman. "You made it! I wasn't sure you'd be able to come."

The woman with the headscarf shrugged lightly. "I cleared my schedule."

The blonde grinned. "Now that you're here, you need to hit the Brownstone Agency tent."

"Really?" The woman tried to keep a smile on her face.

Her friend nodded. "Look, I'll be honest… I went to just get a glimpse of Brownstone, but the food was ridiculously good. Seriously. I was shocked. You'll be kicking yourself if you don't go."

Another man turned toward the women. "I have to agree. I honestly didn't expect much. I mean, the man is a bounty hunter and employs ex-criminals, so I was dubious that they had the finesse to pull it off, but you'd think they'd done nothing but cook barbeque for years. That Brownstone is truly multi-talented."

The woman with the headscarf nodded and turned away. "Brownstone," she hissed under her breath.

Her friend patted her on the shoulder. "Hey, is everything okay?"

"Yes, sorry. Just got a bit lost there for a moment."

James held up the second-place trophy for best sauce. Mack held up the second-place trophy for best beef, and the men all cheered.

Shorty pumped his arm. "*That's* what I'm talking about. We step out the first time, and we're pulling the silver fucking medal. Brownstone Agency *represents*."

Trey frowned and shook his head. "You satisfied with that?"

"What the fuck you talking about, Trey? I thought we was gonna come out here and get our asses handed to us, and instead, we rolling with the big boys, and they all be like, 'Oh, fuck, Brownstone Agency is here, we better run." Shorty snorted. "We got second this time, and we're gonna get first next time, easy."

The other snorted. "We didn't get shit in chicken. How the fuck did we screw up chicken? That shit's easier than beef."

Mack chuckled and shook his head. "Shorty's right. I didn't come here thinking we were even gonna place, so I'm just happy we got anything."

The other men all nodded their agreement, and Trey sighed and shrugged.

James rested the sauce trophy on his shoulder. "I agree with Mack and Shorty. All I have to say to you all is that we might know how to bring in bounties, but barbeque is a whole different level of difficulty."

FINIS

AUTHOR NOTES - MICHAEL ANDERLE

SEPTEMBER 6, 2018

THANK YOU for not only reading this story but these *Author Notes* as well!

After the absolute blast that Alison Brownstone was to create, it was REALLY tempting to do another follow up. However, we have been juggling three (3) series (Brownstone, Shay, and Alison in School) and I can't say that those of us working on these projects think that was such a great idea after all of the headaches it causes.

So, I indulged myself just a little bit and had Alison in the front of this story, and then sent her off to school. But, I am looking forward to the Alison Brownstone project(s) that we will be doing later this year / early 2019.

In this book, I wanted to provide a few fans what they have been waiting for, a balls-to-the-wall type of book. Not much in the way of growth (we touch on it, but hey, that's between all the destruction.) Further, Shay gets a taste of Brownstone's possessiveness.

He is fully capable of allowing her to go charging in,

and has on many occasions. However, sometimes he intends the fight to be just him and the asshole he intends to obliterate.

The Dog, Mike. The Dog...

So, I was talking with Martha Carr about a new project (The Daniel Codex), and she mentioned that there is a nod to *The Unbelievable Mr. Brownstone* in that someone beating up a dog gets their ass handed to them.

The dog lives.

I have no idea how many readers I lost with the murder of James' dog (Leeroy) in book one, but I have received a few comments about it. I personally feel that it was an appropriate death in the book, and helped propel James into an all-out piss-him-off mode that started us down this path where eventually, James adopts a daughter and looks like he might have a full-time woman (wife?) in his future.

Maybe.

Going back to his dog Leeroy, Martha (and others) were warning me that I was going to kill the series right there. Fortunately, you readers forgave me the death of the dog and stayed with me.

I've been thinking about getting James a new dog, now that he has a better home life.

What do you think, do we chance James getting another dog, and if so, what kind? I read reviews, Facebook groups and other places if you want to get the suggestions to me. The ONLY dog I can think he will not get...

...is a Chihuahua.

Ad Aeternitatem,
Michael Anderle

P.S. – *That includes Teacup dogs...not happening. (Editor's note: How about a teacup piglet?)*

Waking Magic (1) - Release of Magic (2) - Protection of Magic (3) - Rule of Magic (4) - Dealing in Magic (5) - Theft of Magic (6) - Enemies of Magic (7) - Guardians of Magic (8)

The Soul Stone Mage Series

* Sarah Noffke and Martha Carr *

House of Enchanted (1) - The Dark Forest (2) - Mountain of Truth (3) - Land of Terran (4) - New Egypt (5) - Lancothy (6) - Virgo (7)

The Kacy Chronicles

* A.L. Knorr and Martha Carr *

Descendant (1) - Ascendant (2) - Combatant (3) - Transcendent (4)

The Midwest Magic Chronicles

* Flint Maxwell and Martha Carr*

The Midwest Witch (1) - The Midwest Wanderer (2) - The Midwest Whisperer (3) - The Midwest War (4)

The Fairhaven Chronicles

* with S.M. Boyce *

Glow (1) - Shimmer (2) - Ember (3) - Nightfall (4)

CONNECT WITH MICHAEL ANDERLE

Michael Anderle Social
  Website:
  http://kurtherianbooks.com/

Email List:
  http://kurtherianbooks.com/email-list/

Facebook Here:
  https://www.facebook.com/OriceranUniverse/
  https://www.
facebook.com/TheKurtherianGambitBooks/

www.ingramcontent.com/pod-product-compliance
Lightning Source LLC
Chambersburg PA
CBHW050235110726
47898CB00007B/2163